SPECIAL MESSAGE TO READERS

**THE ULVERSCROFT FOUNDATION
(registered UK charity number 264873)**
was established in 1972 to provide funds for
research, diagnosis and treatment of eye diseases.
Examples of major projects funded by
the Ulverscroft Foundation are:-

- The Children's Eye Unit at Moorfields Eye Hospital, London
- The Ulverscroft Children's Eye Unit at Great Ormond Street Hospital for Sick Children
- Funding research into eye diseases and treatment at the Department of Ophthalmology, University of Leicester
- The Ulverscroft Vision Research Group, Institute of Child Health
- Twin operating theatres at the Western Ophthalmic Hospital, London
- The Chair of Ophthalmology at the Royal Australian College of Ophthalmologists

You can help further the work of the Foundation
by making a donation or leaving a legacy.
Every contribution is gratefully received. If you
would like to help support the Foundation or
require further information, please contact:

**THE ULVERSCROFT FOUNDATION
The Green, Bradgate Road, Anstey
Leicester LE7 7FU, England
Tel: (0116) 236 4325**

website: www.foundation.ulverscroft.com

DANGEROUS LEGACY

A shocking legacy, from a father she'd always believed was long dead, leads Jenna to Malta and the Hotel Mursaloq. And whilst she is now part owner of the Mursaloq, so too is the handsome Nicholas Portelli. But it quickly becomes apparent that he doesn't welcome her arrival — and soon she is beginning to wonder just how far he will go to rid himself of her . . .

SUSAN UDY

DANGEROUS LEGACY

Complete and Unabridged

LINFORD
Leicester

First published in Great Britain in 2009

First Linford Edition
published 2013

A catalogue record for this book is available
from the British Library.

ISBN 978–1–4448–1543–6

Published by
F. A. Thorpe (Publishing)
Anstey, Leicestershire

Set by Words & Graphics Ltd.
Anstey, Leicestershire
Printed and bound in Great Britain by
T. J. International Ltd., Padstow, Cornwall

This book is printed on acid-free paper

Confronting The Past

Jenna Saliba stood at the bottom of the flight of steps and stared up at the building above; the Hotel Mursaloq. Her legacy — well, 49% of it was.

She couldn't believe it. It was huge. Three storeys high and with a multitude of sliding glass doors behind wrought-iron balconies, it had white walls that were all but smothered in purple bougainvillaea. Immaculately clipped hedges stretched as far as she could see on either side, providing a more or less impenetrable barrier to inquisitive eyes.

As Jenna certainly didn't regard herself as merely inquisitive — it was her right, after all, to see what lay beyond — she stood on her toes to try and see over it. It was no good; the hedge was too high. She could hear the babble of many voices, though; the voice of the guests — her guests, she belatedly realised.

With that, the apprehension that had plagued her on and off from the moment she'd first received the news of her bequest tightened its grip. So much so, that for a split second, she was tempted to turn and run. She didn't, however. Instead, she grabbed her courage with both hands and began to climb the steps, desperately trying to prepare herself for whatever it was that was about to confront her.

It didn't help that she had no idea what to expect once she walked through the tall doors that sat imposingly at the top of the steps. It certainly wasn't a reception area large enough to accommodate the average-size British house twice over and that looked as if it had been lifted straight out of the African jungle.

Tropical plants, vines and palms rampaged on all sides, many of them sending out tentacles long enough to reach a ceiling high above her that ended in an apex and was made entirely of smoked glass. A stream of water cascaded down the length of one stone clad wall into a large pool, the surface of which, she could see, was almost entirely covered in pink and white water lilies.

It made the perfect setting for what she heard next: the unmistakable screech of a parrot. Intrigued, she followed the sound to a large cage and there, on a high perch, sat the brightly hued bird.

'Hello, gorgeous,' it squawked at her. 'Want a kiss?'

It was all Jenna needed. The tension was released and she burst out laughing. 'You're a clever chap. What's your name? Casanova?'

'What's your name?' it stridently repeated.

'Quiet, Columbus,' a voice commanded from behind her.

Startled, Jenna whirled to find herself face to face with a tall — six feet one or two, she estimated — good looking man with bronzed skin. His eyes were deep set and the exact shade of caramel, their expression hooded by heavy lids and a set of lashes that the majority of women would be quite prepared to die for.

He smiled at her, and revealed the coup de grace; a set of flawless white teeth. 'You'll have to excuse him. Or better still, ignore him.'

'Uh — who?' Jenna's mind had become a complete blank in the face of such a handsome individual. Who was he?

'Columbus. He gets totally carried away in the presence of a beautiful woman.'

The colour flamed into Jenna's face. A compliment had been the last thing she'd expected. 'I don't mind,' she told him. 'But why is he speaking English? I mean — he is in Malta — '

'Ah, you've noticed.' His smile widened into a grin. 'That's because, as the majority of our guests are English, that's what he's learnt. Sadly, his remarks aren't always in the best of taste — as you've just heard. For that, I apologise.'

'Oh, please don't. He's adorable and must prove a considerable attraction, saucy or not.'

'He does. Nicholas Portelli, by the way, part-owner of the hotel? How do you do?' He held out his hand, clearly expecting her to return the favour and announce her name as she took it.

But Jenna was struck dumb, as well as being unable to move a single muscle. Nicholas Portelli! This was Nicholas Portelli? She'd been expecting a man twice his age. All that she'd heard to date had suggested that. Her breath hissed through her teeth. Good grief! How was she supposed to operate with this — this vision in front of her at every turn?

'Um . . . ' she stuttered, 'I — I'm — Helen, um — Helen Carne.' She couldn't tell him who she really was, not yet. She needed time to get used to all that had transpired before anyone here knew who she was. Especially

Nicholas Portelli. The only name she'd been able to think of in her panic was her mother's maiden name.

Her hand, when she did finally manage to proffer it, trembled in his. Mainly because she wasn't accustomed to duplicity. It was a tendency that she'd always despised in others, and now, here she was, guilty of just that. Would he notice? Wonder why she was shaking? Worse than that, would he guess who she was?

But apparently not, because all he said was, 'Nice to meet you, Ms Carne.' He smiled again and the caramel-coloured eyes warmed until they looked more like the dark treacle toffee she remembered from her childhood. They also crinkled attractively at the corners. Jenna felt her breathing quicken. 'Are you staying here?'

Desperately, she strove for calm. She was going to have to eventually work with this man if everything went according to plan. And how was she going to do that if she was permanently under his spell? It was imperative she control herself, start as she meant to go on. Her resolve, however, came to nothing.

'Um — no. I — that is ... ' She sounded a complete fool. *Get a grip, Jenna.* she told herself.

He tilted his head to one side; a strand of hair dropped forward, caressing his brow. Jenna's fingers itched to smooth it back.

'No, I'm staying a couple of miles away, but I might move in a day or two. I was just checking out some of the hotels in the area. Not that there's anything wrong with ... ' She was beginning to witter. Something she did when nervous.

'I see.' He clearly didn't, however. If the small frown that belatedly tugged at his brow was anything to go by.

She nibbled at her lower lip. Something else she only did in times of stress. She should have told him her real name. What was he going to think when she eventually came clean? Which she would have to, and sooner rather than later. What else could he think, in the wake of her stuttering performance, but that she was witless? And a liar to boot. It wasn't an alluring prospect. And certainly not the way to embark upon any relationship, business or otherwise.

'Well,' he was still holding her hand, 'let's hope we meet again in a day or two. You'll be most welcome. We do still have one or two rooms vacant so . . . '

'Oh, right — yes.' She couldn't mistake his meaning, he was implying that she shouldn't wait too long before checking in. She eased her hand out of his.

'I have to get on. Sightseeing to do, you know.' What was the matter with her? She knew perfectly well what was the matter with her. He was. He was the exact opposite of everything she'd been expecting. For starters, he was about forty years too young. And way, way too good looking.

'Your first visit to Malta?' he asked.

'Yes, it is.'

'First impressions?' He was grinning at her again, the perfect white teeth on full view, the embodiment of amiability and charm. Did the man have no faults at all?

'Oh, good, good. Yes, definitely good.' She clamped her lips together.

'Splendid. Well, I hope to see you soon, Ms Carne.'

'Yes, I'm sure you will.' And with that, she turned and bolted through the doors, trying to ignore the prickling sensation that pair of treacle-dark eyes remorselessly boring into her back induced.

★　★　★

It wasn't until she was seated in a taxi, and halfway back to her hotel in Mellieha, that she managed to banish Nicholas Portelli from her mind and allow it to return to her reasons for being here, in Malta. Not that those particular thoughts had been absent for any length of time — not since the moment when she'd first clapped eyes on those fateful words.

Her initial reaction that day had been to stare blankly at the newspaper that her closest friend, Pauline, had thrust at her, with no inkling of the dramatic events that were about to unfold around her. When was it? Just under a fortnight ago? It felt more like six months, so much had happened since.

'Look — look at that,' Pauline had said excitedly, jabbing her finger at a boxed advertisement. 'It's your mum — someone's trying to find her. There can't be another Helen with that surname, not here in Birmingham. It must be her.'

Jenna read the words printed inside the box. *HELEN SALIBA, wife of Vincent Saliba. Please contact solicitor, Stella Delaney, at Honeyrigg, Bennett and Delaney at . . .* and there followed a Birmingham address and phone number . . . *where she will hear something to her advantage.*

'What do you think it's about?' Pauline's eyes were alight with curiosity and speculation. Not surprisingly, Helen had been dead now for five years. Vince had been gone much longer. Who could be searching for her mother after all this time?

'Haven't a clue,' Jenna replied, her brow wrinkling as she read and re-read the words.

'Well, there's only one way to find out.'

'What?' Jenna regarded her friend absently, her mind still on the intriguing words . . . *something to her advantage.* Didn't such words usually indicate a legacy of some sort? But who could have died? And surely, if they were close enough to Helen to leave her something in their will, they'd have known she was dead?

'Ring the number.'

'Oh, yeah — right.'

'Well, go on then.' And Pauline gave her a gentle push.

11

Jenna didn't move. She couldn't. She felt incapable of the smallest step. Her heart rate had doubled and the strangest feeling was coming over her. A feeling that her life was about to change, for ever.

'Go on,' Pauline again urged, impatiently this time, 'I'll cover for you if old Mortimer comes along.' Old Mortimer was the manager of J. L. Keeley's, the department store in which they both worked, and had the uncanny knack of turning up at precisely the wrong moment; some sort of inbuilt radar, Pauline always maintained, set to pick up any kind of misdemeanour on the part of his staff.

'OK.' Jenna obediently headed for the staff room, her hazel eyes still riveted to the words that were printed on the sheet of newspaper. It couldn't be a mistake. As Pauline had pointed out, it was extremely unlikely that there would be another Helen Saliba here in Birmingham, or anywhere else in the country, come to that.

Once inside the staff room, she pulled out her mobile phone and, with fingers that quivered, pressed in the numbers of the firm of solicitors.

It all happened very quickly after that. She spoke to some sort of secretary, she presumed, and was given an appointment for the next day, her day off as luck would have it.

She took a taxi to the address that had been given in the paper — Pauline had insisted on that, although Jenna was quite prepared to hop on to the bus as she usually did.

'Treat yourself, gal,' Pauline had cried. 'For all you know, you could be the possessor of a huge fortune.'

Jenna wasn't so sure of that. It all seemed very peculiar. She didn't know anyone wealthy enough to leave any sort of legacy behind them. And she was pretty sure her mother hadn't either. She'd tried to question the secretary, but the woman had clammed up instantly.

'Miss Delaney will apprise you of all the facts,' she'd primly said. So Jenna was still none the wiser about the reason for the advert. She just hoped she wasn't wasting her precious day off on a wild goose chase.

The taxi driver dropped her outside a red brick Victorian building on the outskirts of the city centre. She went inside and within moments was being shown into an office to find herself face to face with a woman that she presumed was Stella Delaney.

The solicitor looked at her with sympathy. Jenna had informed the person who'd answered the phone the day before that her mother was dead. Clearly that information had been passed on.

'I'm very sorry about your mother, Miss Saliba.'

'Thank you.'

The solicitor paused then. 'I'm also sorry to be the bearer of further bad news.'

Jenna felt her heart lurch.

'Your father's solicitor, Max Pollacco, was left instructions along with your father's will to find you and your mother.' She glanced at some papers on her desk. 'Your father had a partner, Nicholas Portelli . . . '

Jenna held up a hand, halting the flow of words. 'Just a moment. My father's solicitor? Max? Max who? And partner? What partner? I don't understand.' Her mother had never mentioned a partner. And with a name like Nicholas Portelli she certainly would have remembered it if she had. And why would her father's solicitor leave it this long to get in touch? Surely he couldn't have been looking for her mother all this time? 'When was this?'

'A week ago.'

'A week ago!' She shook her head. 'My father died twenty years ago. In a road accident after he left my mother and me,' she blurted. 'Why has it taken so long for . . . '

'Twenty years ago? No, Miss Saliba,

that's not correct. Let me just check.'
Stella glanced down at a paper on her
desk, her brow knitted with concern.
'Your father was Vincent Saliba of the
Hotel Mursaloq in Malta? In the North
West of the island.'

Jenna stared at her. 'He was called
Vincent Saliba, yes, and he was
Maltese, but as I've just said,' she too
now frowned, 'he left us and — and he
was killed. And I've never heard of the
Hotel Mursaloq. This can't be right. It
can't be the same man. It must be some
sort of weird coincidence.' She started
to get to her feet.

She had wasted her time on a wild
goose chase. Pauline was wrong. As
unlikely as it seemed, there must, after
all, be another Helen Saliba and
Vincent. It wasn't her mother that the
solicitors were seeking, Saliba was
probably a common name on Malta.

But the solicitor's voice stopped her.
'Would you have a look at this, please?
It should confirm whether Vincent
Saliba is your father or not.' And she

16

pulled out a photograph from amongst the papers. 'Is this your mother? Helen Saliba?'

Jenna took it from her and stared at it. It was unmistakably her mother, a much younger Helen it was true, but, nonetheless, it was Helen. Jenna nodded.

'Miss Saliba, sadly, I have to inform you that your father died just two weeks ago.' She fell silent for a second or two, as she studied Jenna carefully, curiously. 'Who told you he'd been killed twenty years ago?'

'M-my mother.'

The solicitor regarded her curiously. 'Whatever made your mother believe that?'

'I don't know.' Jenna sat down again. She had to. She was in imminent danger of collapse. What on earth was going on here?

'Well, I don't like to suggest such a thing, but . . . ' she paused, as if she were indeed reluctant to put her thoughts into words. Jenna felt a stab of misgiving. What was coming now? She'd had a big enough shock just learning that for the past twenty years her father had been alive, when all the time she'd believed him dead, never mind being forced to hear yet more shocking news, 'could she have had some reason to lie to you?'

Jenna stared at the solicitor, her expression a mixture of shock and outrage at the solicitor's suggestion. 'Why would she do that? What possible reason could she have had?'

The solicitor shrugged. 'Maybe in the circumstances that you've just mentioned.'

Jenna stared at her enquiringly.

'Your father leaving? Well, I wondered — could it maybe have been to stop you asking about him? Wanting to see him? I mean, if you believed he was dead.' She shrugged again. 'You wouldn't ask to see him, maybe? I don't know. And it depends, I suppose, on the circumstances under which he left. Maybe he threatened her?'

'Threatened her? With what?' Jenna's voice rose, almost hysterically. 'Violence? What? What are you suggesting?' She was appalled; outraged. How dare this woman say such a thing? What she recalled of her father was that he had been a gentle man. She couldn't ever remember him raising his voice to her, let alone his hand. Although — but she blanked those thoughts from her mind. She couldn't — wouldn't consider that now. Not now.

'No, no, of course I'm not suggesting violence. But supposing he threatened to take you with him? And you wanted to go? Presumably you loved your father?'

'Well, yes, but I loved my mother too — and I was only three.'

'Of course. But do you remember asking to see him?'

'Well . . . yes.'

'Did he threaten to take you with him?'

'I don't know.' Jenna pressed the palm of her hand to her forehead. She

19

had to think. She'd been so young. An image of a tall, grey haired man manifested itself, a soft voice calling her.

But the solicitor's voice went on, driving away those thoughts.

'Well, if he did, she might have wanted to prevent any further contact between you and the best way to do that would be to tell you he was dead and then move you both somewhere else. He wouldn't know where you were then and so wouldn't be able to keep in touch with you. These are just guesses, you understand. I really don't know. But your mother must have had some reason to tell you such a thing.' She studied Jenna's face anxiously. 'Clearly, you've had no contact with him since.'

Jenna didn't respond; she couldn't. She did manage to shake her head. None of it made sense. None of it. Yet one thing was irrefutable. If her father hadn't been killed in a road accident then her mother must have lied. But why? Why would she do that?

Or could she genuinely have believed her husband to be dead? Could it all have been some sort of ghastly mistake? That's what Jenna badly wanted to believe. Anything but that her mother had deliberately let her think her beloved father was dead. But surely, as his wife, she would have been asked to identify the body? And if not, why not?

Jenna pressed both hands to her mouth now, to hide the small sob that involuntarily erupted from her. It was all too much to take in. And her father owned a hotel by the sound of it, or had owned a hotel. On Malta.

★   ★   ★

Jenna had been just three years old when her father had disappeared from their lives. She did dimly recall repeatedly asking her mother where her daddy had gone and Helen prevaricating. He'd gone away to work had been the most often used excuse and, naturally, at just three years old, Jenna

21

had unquestioningly accepted that. Accepted that he never came home as other children's fathers did.

It wasn't until some years later, she'd been six or seven and she'd started pressing her mother to see Vince, to go and find him, that Helen had told her that he had left them and then, sometime later, she wasn't sure how long exactly, wasn't sure even if Helen had said, been knocked down by a car. It had been a considerable shock because Jenna had lived with the hope, and faith, that her father would one day return.

As young as she was, she'd realised then that that was why they'd never heard anything further from him. Mind you, they had moved around an awful lot in the previous three years, from one rented flat in the suburbs of Birmingham to another, so she'd decided that he would have had considerable difficulty keeping track of them in any case. They'd never stayed anywhere for longer than six months. Sometimes it was a much shorter time than that.

It had been very disruptive for Jenna, allowing her no time to make any real friends. Even her mother hadn't seemed to have any friends, or if she had, she hadn't brought them home. It would have meant she could keep her address a secret from everyone, and there'd be no chance of her husband ever finding her. But if that were true, why had she been so against him having contact with them both? Jenna, in particular? Could Stella Delaney be right? And he had threatened to take her with him?

She couldn't remember him ever saying that, though. But then, as she hadn't seen him, she supposed she wouldn't. She presumed he'd been in contact with her mother at least initially, although she wasn't even sure of that. Why hadn't she asked her mother more questions while she could? Why?

Pauline was Jenna's first real friend and she hadn't met her until four years ago when they'd both started work at

J. L. Keeley's. Helen had always told Jenna they were moving for a better job, more money. But neither the better job nor the extra money ever materialised. In fact, they'd lived more or less from hand to mouth.

Jenna looked at Stella now. There was something else she desperately needed to know. 'Do you know, did my father try and find us . . . me before? While he was alive?'

Stella looked at her, her expression once more one of deep sympathy. 'I really don't know. Sorry, if you'll have to ask someone else about that. Max Pollacco or Mr Portelli, perhaps. I do know that the last address he had for you both was in Birmingham, but when that was, I couldn't say. Anyway, it was decided to start trying to contact Mrs Saliba here in Birmingham.'

'Do you know how my father died? Was he ill?'

'I'm sorry, I don't know. I was just asked to try and find your mother.'

Jenna struggled to take it all in. 'And

this, this Mr Portelli?'

'Nicholas Portelli, yes. As I said, he was your father's partner in the hotel, Miss Saliba.'

'Jenna, please.'

The solicitor smiled at her. 'Jenna. Your father left your mother his half of the hotel — well, 49% to be exact. Your mother would have inherited that plus £125,000 if she'd still been alive. Now, of course, it will automatically go to you. Mr Saliba stipulated that in his will. In the event of both parties, you and your mother, being deceased, both the 49% of the hotel and the money would have gone to Nicholas Portelli.'

Whatever Jenna had expected to hear today, it hadn't been this.

'According to Mr Pollacco, Mr Portelli is willing to buy your share of the hotel. Price subject to negotiation, naturally. I would advise you, in these rather unusual circumstances, to accept his offer.'

'No. I'm not agreeing to anything. Not yet. I'm going to Malta to see the hotel for myself. I also want to discover more about my father and I can only do that there. All I know is that approximately thirty years ago he came to England from Malta to work and almost immediately met my mother. They married and had me.' Her voice broke as tears filled her eyes and throat.

'You're very young, Jenna,' the solicitor began gently.

'I'm twenty-three.'

The solicitor appeared surprised. Jenna wasn't. People invariably under-estimated her age. Must be something to do with her heart shaped face, her dimpled cheeks and her girlish figure.

'I see. Well, if you're sure?'

'I am.'

'In that case, I'll notify Max Pollacco that we've found you.'

'I'd rather you didn't, not just yet.'

Stella Delaney looked doubtful. 'Jenna, I can't agree to that — code of ethics and all that.'

'Please. I'd rather just turn up, have a

look round before anyone knows who I am.'

Stella Delaney looked even more doubtful, to the point of shaking her head.

'OK. Tell him you've found me, but I won't tell you when I'm planning to go there. That way, you can honestly say you don't know. It's just — well, I'll get a better idea of things, of people, if they don't know who I am. I mean everyone puts on an act, don't they? And there's no urgency about things any more. My father's dead.'

Jenna Says Goodbye

That proved to be a huge source of grief to Jenna over the following days. She'd have given everything she possessed to have seen her father again before he died. They could have spent some time together, getting to know each other. If he'd been ill, she could have nursed him. She had her memories of him, naturally, but they were a small child's memories and not very clear.

She thought she recalled a tall, slender man, with a gentle smile and a shock of grey hair. She did remember him playing with her, lifting her up and throwing her in the air. She also recalled the bewilderment when one day he didn't come home from work. She'd gone to bed one evening, he'd taken her up, read to her, cuddled and kissed her, and then the next day he wasn't there.

From that time on, it was just her mother and her, constantly moving. The sheer loneliness, the insecurity of it made her very unhappy. She loved her mother, but she needed her father too. She desperately wanted to be like all the other children she knew, the ones whose fathers took them to the park, took them swimming, met them occasionally from school, attended school events. But then came the day when Helen told her he was dead. She'd cried endlessly, her mother had been quite unable to comfort her, console her.

One question nagged at her ceaselessly. Why had her mother told her he was dead? The more Jenna had thought about it, the more convinced she became that Helen had lied to her.

Evidently he'd returned to his homeland, Malta, but surely he could have tried to keep in touch? It was hardly on the other side of the world. He'd loved her, she had no doubt of that. So what had gone wrong?

She needed answers, but with her mother dead too, there was no-one to ask. Unless . . . there was her god-mother, Rosemary. She'd taken Jenna in when her mother died, Jenna, at just eighteen, being too young to live alone. Even though, for years Rosemary hadn't had the faintest idea where they were.

Although, she had told Jenna at one point, after she'd moved in with her, that several years before, someone, a man, had come asking for their address. As they'd moved on by then, Rosemary, of course, couldn't provide any information. She'd had no idea who he'd been and he had refused to say why he wanted to know.

Jenna had thought it strange when Rosemary told her, but had swiftly forgotten about it. Now, she wondered if her father had sent him? But, if that were the case, why hadn't the person been willing to reveal who he was and who had sent him? If it had indeed been her father searching for them?

Undaunted by the likelihood that Rosemary would know no more than she did, she picked up the phone and keyed in her godmother's number.

'Rosemary Stanton speaking.'

'It's Jenna.'

'Oh, how lovely, Jenna. How are you, dear? It's been months since I heard from you. Are you still in the same flat?'

A wave of guilt engulfed Jenna. 'Sorry. Um — no, I moved. I'm sharing now with a friend. I should have let you know, sorry.'

'Don't be. I know what you young things can be like.'

Jenna could hear her smile in the gentle words. Rosemary had been a rock to the young girl, had stood by her, supported her both emotionally and financially.

Jenna told Rosemary all that had transpired.

'Oh, my goodness.' The older woman sounded as astonished as Jenna had been by news of her father's recent death and subsequent will, so clearly

Rosemary wouldn't be able to tell her anything. Jenna's hopes were dashed. 'I had no idea, my dear. Your mother told me he'd left suddenly . . . with another woman she said, but I had my doubts about that. He adored Helen. Anyway, some time later she said he'd been killed in a road accident. So, he went back to Malta,' she mused.

Another woman? That was news to Jenna. Why hadn't her mother ever mentioned it? Maybe not when Jenna was a mere three years old, but surely once she was older Helen could have said something? At least it provided some sort of explanation as to why Vince had left them so suddenly.

If it was true, that is. If her mother had indeed lied about his death, maybe she'd lied about that too? Maybe she hadn't wanted to admit that he'd simply upped and left? Maybe she'd considered it a failure on her part, the fact that she'd been unable to make him happy enough to stay? Or maybe something she'd done had driven him away? Something she was ashamed of?

'Did she ever identify his body?'

'I don't think so. She certainly never mentioned it, but then, if he wasn't really killed she wouldn't have done. Why on earth would she have said such a thing?'

'I wondered if it had been a case of mistaken identity and she really did believe my father was dead. If she hadn't actually seen the body.'

'Oh, my dear, I really couldn't say. It's all very strange. Your mother did swear me to secrecy about the other woman, she didn't want you to know, and, well, once I'd heard he'd been killed it no longer seemed important.'

* * *

More than ever determined now to go to Malta and discover for herself what her father had been doing for the past twenty years and, even more importantly, to try and uncover his reasons for leaving them . . . leaving her, Jenna wasted no time booking a flight.

She received a letter from Max Pollacco, asking whether she would be flying out to Malta and when, so obviously Stella had notified him of her whereabouts. She didn't reply. She excused her bad manners by telling herself that she'd be out there before a letter arrived.

She handed in her notice at the store. Pauline was desolate at the news of her imminent departure and the fact that she'd most likely be staying in Malta. 'What am I going to do without you? I wish I'd never shown you that advert.' I never dreamt you'd leave the country for good. I'm going to have to find another flatmate,' she finally wailed.

'You can come out and see me. Malta's not the other side of the world,' was Jenna's response to all of this.

'I might take you up on your invitation to fly out.' Pauline eyed her then, her natural nosiness taking over from her distress. 'Wonder what this

Nicholas Portelli's like? Did your solicitor say?'

'Nothing, but I would imagine he's about the same age as my father.'

'Hmmm. Then again, he could be young, impossibly handsome.'

'Yeah, yeah. Dream on. With my luck, he'll probably turn out to be even older than my father was . . . '

Her voice broke with the realisation of all she'd missed. If she'd known her father had been alive, she'd have moved heaven and earth to find him.

* * *

If Pauline was upset at Jenna leaving, Rick Colby, her boyfriend, was devastated. That and furiously angry.

'It's all a bit sudden, isn't it?' he exclaimed.

'Well, yes, but as I didn't know my father was alive, much less back on Malta and owner of half a hotel.'

'For goodness sake, Jenna, have you thought this through? It's a huge step to take. I mean, what do you know about Malta? You could hate it.'

'Or look at it more positively, I might love it. It's a huge gamble, I freely admit, but I have to go. Don't you see that? I've thought about it very carefully and I'm as certain as I can be that it's the right thing to do; the only thing to do. I owe it to my father to see where he ended his life.'

'Why? He didn't care about you, obviously,' Rick blurted out, 'otherwise he'd have come back to see you.'

'He wouldn't have know where I was, we moved around so much,' she told him, trying to disregard his cruel remark.

He didn't mean it, he was hurting — every bit as much at the possibility of losing her as she was at losing her father, a father whom she'd never been given the chance to know.

'He'd have wanted me to go.' If only she were as confident as she sounded. The truth was — over the past day or so, the doubts had flared

up in their thousands; insistent, unde-
niable. Making her all too aware that
she was giving up everything here to
journey to an unknown island. Making
her ask — what if things didn't work
out in Malta?

'I thought we had something good
going. Something that would last. I love
you, Jenna. You must know that!'

Jenna hadn't realised he'd felt like
that. She really hadn't. Oh, she liked
Rick well enough, but deep down, she
knew he wasn't the one, the love of her
life. He was good company and they'd
had fun together, but that's all it had
been. In fact, she'd already been
thinking of ending things and this
provided the perfect excuse. She'd have
ended it before if she'd realised how
seriously he was beginning to take it all.

'Well, we did — do have a good
relationship, but . . . '

'But what?' he angrily demanded.

'You know as well as I do, Rick, it
isn't really love, you would have told me
before if it was.'

'Don't tell me what I know. Just because I've never said it, it doesn't mean I don't feel it. I was just waiting for the right time. I didn't want to rush you.'

'Oh, Rick, I'm sorry.'

'Yeah, it looks like it. You can't wait to go, can you?'

She couldn't deny that and didn't even try. But they eventually parted on reasonably good terms, even though Jenna knew she'd hurt him deeply.

★ ★ ★

So it was that ten days after her meeting with the solicitor, Jenna boarded a plane for Malta. As she sat gazing through the small window, she wondered, for the umpteenth time, if she was quite, quite mad? Rick had certainly thought she was.

To abandon a whole way of life, a job, friends, to fly off to a Mediterranean island, with no concept of the difficulties, the opposition, even, that she might have to face when she got there. After all, Nicholas Portelli might be aghast at having to content with a partner many years his junior, and could, if he was so minded, place all sorts of obstacles in her way.

But whatever her doubts, she was all too quickly stepping from the plane to be enfolded in the breathtaking heat of Luqa airport, from where a taxi cab transported her to a small hotel on the edge of Mellieha.

She'd decided not to go directly to the Hotel Mursaloq. She'd belatedly realised that she would have to give her real name when checking in and, as she'd said to solicitor, she wished to remain incognito for a couple of days. That way she could visit her father's hotel and have a look round with no-one any the wiser. Maybe even snatch a glimpse of Nicholas Portelli. It would give her much needed time to consider whether she could, after all, remain in Malta and become a full working partner in the hotel.

The landscape that surrounded her on the journey from the airport was all that the photographs in the many travel brochures that she'd minutely studied had promised. There it all was, laid out before her: the sun baked soil, the Moorish style buildings, the tropical foliage and flowers, the diamond-speckled, turquoise sea, the periwinkle-blue sky.

It was all terribly exciting, and, for the moment at least, she felt like any other tourist. With the intimidating prospect of confronting Nicholas Portelli several comforting days away. Nonetheless, on more than one occasion, she found herself praying that he would turn out to be as attractive and likeable as the landscape that surrounded her, and, more importantly, that he would like her.

* * *

The following morning, feeling refreshed and considerably calmer after a good night's sleep, she decided to take her first look at the hotel of which she now owned 49%. And that was how she'd encountered Nicholas Portelli.

Sitting alone over dinner that same evening, she acknowledged that she could procrastinate no longer. She had to come clean and make herself known. Her heart gave an almighty lurch at the prospect, inducing a feeling of nausea and extreme uncertainty. It was too soon. She'd hoped for another couple of days, at least, before having to endure what she increasingly suspected would be an ordeal.

Nicholas Portelli had turned out to be nothing like she had imagined and what on earth was he going to think of her after her deception over her name the Lord alone knew. Still, it had to be done, so the sooner she did it, the better.

The very next morning she again took a taxi cab and this time nervously presented herself to the pretty receptionist of the Hotel Mursaloq.

'I-I'd like t-to speak to Nicholas Portelli if that's possible,' she haltingly said. She bit at her bottom lip. She sounded like an agitated schoolgirl, being sent to see the head in the wake of some terrible misdemeanour.

'What is your name, please?'

Jenna hesitated, but then decided to stick with her mother's maiden name, just until she'd declared herself to Nicholas. She didn't want anyone to know she was here before he did, she owed him that much. And who knew how much this girl knew? She might know nothing, but then again she might know everything.

'I'll just see if he's free.'

The girl murmured into the phone and then turned to Jenna and said, 'He'll see you now.' She indicated a door on the far side of the reception area. 'Through there, please.'

A weird sensation of relief mixed with deep apprehension afflicted Jenna then. The moment of truth. How would Nicholas greet her declaration? With relief that she'd been found? Or with anger at her initial deceit?

Timidly, she knocked on his door and, at the sound of his, 'Enter,' went inside to confront her destiny — whatever it might turn out to be.

A Disturbing Confrontation

Nicholas Portelli was sitting at a desk writing, but, upon her entrance, looked up and smiled — just as he had the day before when he'd introduced himself to her.

'Hello again. This is a nice surprise.' He stood up and walked around the desk. 'What can I do for you? Have you decided to give us the pleasure of having you to stay? I'm sure there's still a room available. He lifted the phone, presumably to speak to the reception desk and verify this.

'I'm — um, I'm J-Jenna Saliba,' she burst out before he could do so.

His smile disappeared and his hand froze in mid-air as he stared at her, a puzzled frown lowering his brow. 'But, sorry, I thought you said you were

44

Helen Carne.' Then it was as if the reality of what she'd said sank in and the frown deepened. He slowly replaced the phone. 'You mean you're Vince's daughter.' He paused, then, 'I don't understand.' He shook his head slightly. 'Why the false name? The secrecy? It suggests you have something to hide.'

'Not really.' She heard the tremble in her voice and wondered if he did. Maybe if he did, he'd realise how nervous she was and that that terrible coldness would disappear from his face, his eyes.

It didn't. In fact, if anything his expression of contempt had deepened, which did seem a little over the top. She'd only told a small lie about her name, after all. It was hardly a sin.

'So,' his voice was now as scathing as his look. 'Maybe you'd like to explain why neither you, nor your mother while she was still alive, had any contact with Vince until now, of course, when he's dead and you stand to inherit a considerable amount of money, as well as virtually half of his hotel?'

Jenna gasped in horror. This was even worse than she'd expected. Nothing could have prepared her for it. It did, however, explain the expression of contempt. The blood chilled in her veins, making her shiver, despite the warmth of the room.

'How do I know you're who you say you are?' he then demanded.

'Ring Stella Delaney. She'll vouch for me. And,' she pulled her passport from her bag. 'Here's my passport.'

He took it from her and opened it to her photograph.

'Right.' He thrust it back at her.

'And just for the record,' she snapped, partially recovering, at least, her equilibrium. After all, what right did this man have to make such a snap, and mistaken, judgement about her? Her anger started to rise, effectively banishing the chilling mortification of a moment ago when he'd made it abundantly clear that he believed her to be nothing more than a heartless gold-digger, 'I didn't give you my real name because . . . '

'Well, do go on. Because?' His tone was the coldest thing she'd ever heard.

She gulped. She'd brought this on herself with her stupid lie. Whatever had she been thinking of? She ploughed on, desperately trying to ignore the scorn that now twisted his lips, desperate to somehow vindicate herself. 'Because I wanted to find out about all of this . . . ' she indicated the hotel in general with a sweep of her hand, 'before anyone knew who I was. I hadn't expected to meet you. I — I just needed a little time, that's all — sorry — ' Her words limped into silence. 'It's all been a shock,' she lamely finished.

'And have you had it?' he harshly demanded to know.

'What?' Jenna blinked at him. 'A shock? I've just said . . . ' She was confused. Not surprisingly. The last thing she'd expected was to be accused of gold-digging.

'The time. Have you had it?'

'Not really.'

'Then, why confess?' There was a merciless glitter to his eye now, and an even more unpleasant edge to his voice. 'I mean you could have gone on playing games for days yet and no-one would have been any the wiser. What fun it would have been. Fooling everyone.'

Jenna ignored that last gibe. 'Because I thought I should — after meeting you yesterday.'

He continued to narrowly eye her, his face still an unyielding mask. He was never going to forgive her for this. What a start to their working relationship. She'd more than likely succeeded in wrecking things before they'd even begun.

'I see. But I'm wondering now, did Stella Delaney agree to this, this deception?'

'No. Please,' Jenna broke in. Things were going from bad to worse. 'Don't blame Stella. It's entirely down to me, all of this. She didn't know when I intended travelling here as I didn't tell her. As I've just said, I wanted to have a couple of days here before anyone knew who I was. And I wouldn't exactly describe it as deception,' she said miserably.

'Oh would you not?' His one eyebrow zoomed upwards. 'What would you describe it as then?'

Jenna remained silent. There didn't seem much she could say. He was right. It was deception, there was no other word for it. Maybe she should simply jump on to the next plane back to England, because she didn't see how they could possibly work together after this. He would never trust her again. And, in all fairness, how could she blame him?

'So, tell me, why did you never get in touch with your father while he was still alive? Visit him? Why wait till now?' He wasn't quite shouting at her but it was obvious he was furiously angry. 'Both you and your mother knew where he was? I know for a fact that he wrote. Do you have any idea how much your neglect grieved him?'

'No, of course I don't. I thought he was dead. I thought he'd died almost twenty years ago.'

'What? Oh please, not more lies!' He was practically shouting at her now.

Jenna's eyes flashed her fury, even though she accepted that he had good reason to doubt anything she said. 'I'm not lying. I wouldn't lie about something like that, despite what you might think of me. And, for your information, he didn't write. I never ever saw a letter from him, and I'm sure if there had been one my mother would have showed me,' her distress at his unjust accusations was starting to show, her voice shook. 'She knew how upset I was at his leaving, she couldn't have known where he was, she couldn't have!'

Nicholas Portelli made no response to that, he simply waited for her to go on.

'My mother told me he'd been killed in a motor accident. I was six years old at the time. I believed her. Why wouldn't I have? I didn't see any letter,' she said, as if by repeating it, she could compel him to believe her, just as she'd believed her mother all those years ago.

But Nicholas's eyes only narrowed even further, his lips tightened. 'Why would she tell you he was dead? She must have known he wasn't.'

'I have no idea. Don't you think if I'd — I'd known he was alive, I'd have made sure I saw him?' Her eyes were stinging now with hot tears, they laced her words, thickening them.

Angry with herself for this display of weakness in front of this hard faced man, she dashed them away. How could she have been attracted to him? His face was set in rigid lines, the muscles standing out in his jawline, his eyes menacing slits.

And, all of a sudden, his expression softened and his glacial eyes warmed. Had he realised she was frightened of him? 'Well, she clearly didn't want to be found so she must have deliberately lied to you.'

It was what she'd dreaded hearing. 'Wh-why do you say that?'

'Because every time he thought he'd located the two of you, and that was quite a few times, she would vanish again. Believe me, she knew only too well that he was alive and looking for you both. And she took steps to ensure he never found you. In the end, he gave up. It broke his heart.'

The knowledge that her father had searched for them, for her, had wanted to keep in touch, despatched a sensation of utter joy through Jenna. This was immediately followed by an explosion of such grief that he hadn't found them, it almost felled her right where she stood.

'Why would she do that? She knew how much I loved him.'

Could, as Stella Delaney had seemed at one point to be suggesting, Helen have been frightened of Vince? At the time, Jenna had angrily dismissed the possibility. But now, as little as she wanted to, she considered the question once more. Could Vince have been a violent husband? She couldn't think of any other reason for her mother keeping him from his daughter.

'Well, clearly none of it was your fault. You were far too young at the time to comprehend what was happening. Although, you must have wondered, as you got older, why you moved around so much? Did you never ask your mother why?'

'Yes, of course I did, but she always said it was for a job. And — and again, I believed her. Why wouldn't I? I had no reason to think otherwise.'

'I don't understand why she told you Vince was dead.' He regarded her thoughtfully, speculatively even; the initial contempt and anger wiped clean. 'Unless it was to stop you trying to eventually contact him? Could be that she was afraid he'd go for custody and take you away from her?' He was echoing Stella's words. At least, he wasn't suggesting some sort of violence. For that, at least, she could be grateful.

'Although, I don't believe for a second that Vince would have done that. He was such a gentle man.' His voice deepened, momentarily. 'He was broken-hearted when he failed to trace you. He loved you very much. Just as he still seemed to love your mother. Otherwise why leave his entire wealth to her? That doesn't suggest a man who hated his wife, or even bore her a grudge.'

An involuntary sob escaped Jenna at that. At the thought of all that she'd missed. The chance of knowing her father, the father she remembered loving very much, as young as she'd been. But a small frown puckered her brow. If her father had still loved her mother, as Nicholas seemed to think, why had he left her for another woman? It didn't make sense. Maybe Nicholas could tell her?

'Do you know, did he have anyone with him when he arrived in Malta? A woman?'

'A woman?' Nicholas shook his head. 'I don't think so. But then, Vince was a very private man. Why?'

'My godmother told me that my mother said he ran off with a woman.'

'There was no woman on the scene when I first met him, let's see, it must be seventeen, eighteen years ago, or since as far as I know. I suppose there could have been before that. If there had been someone, he kept her very much to himself.

'Of course, there must have been women over the years, he was a normal, red blooded man, after all, but I wasn't aware of anyone special. And, as he was a friend of my parents, I think I would have known. They would have known, certainly, and talked about her, met her, in all probability. Vince and my parents became close friends.'

So, if there had been someone, she evidently hadn't come to Malta with him. Or if she had, the affair hadn't lasted because as Nicholas said, surely he would have known about it? Even though he would have been little more than a boy at the time.

'I asked Stella Delaney but she didn't know. How did my father die?'

'Cancer. Sadly, he'd left things too late, there was nothing they could do. It was relatively quick — six months.'

Jenna gasped, lifting a hand to her mouth to hide its quiver. 'I would have come if I'd known.'

Just for a second, his eyes warmed and softened. 'He'd have been pleased to know that. However, on a lighter note, can I assume you'll be moving in here now?' Nicholas went on to ask, clearly trying to ease the sadness.

'Yes. I'll go and collect my things and come straight back.'

'I'll call a taxi for you, and then perhaps, this evening, you'll have dinner with me — in my apartment? You will, of course, stay in your father's apartment for as long as you wish. They're both on the top floor, next door to each other.'

It didn't take Jenna long to fetch her

belongings and return. She'd brought very little with her to Malta, having given most of her possessions away. Nicholas was nowhere to be seen, so she collected the key to the apartment from the pretty receptionist, who clearly was expecting her, and made her own way up to the apartment that had been her father's home for so many years.

★ ★ ★

Jenna gasped with pleasure when she saw it. With rooms that faced the sea, the apartment felt airy and spacious. This impression was accentuated by the fact that every window was extremely wide and stretched from floor to ceiling, with sliding doors that opened on to a balcony, a balcony that was much larger than the ones she'd initially viewed from outside the hotel.

The apartment comprised a magnificently fitted kitchen, a sitting-cum-dining room that could have easily contained the entire flat that she shared with Pauline, an equally large bedroom and an en-suite bathroom to die for, all bronze and dark green marble, with gold accessories and a sunken bath.

Her father had clearly done extremely well for himself. A surge of pride went through her. If only she could have known him. Spent some time here with him. Let him know how very much she loved him.

A deep sadness engulfed her. For all that she'd been denied, as well as for whatever reasons her mother had had for doing that. Because the more she considered her mother's actions, the more she concluded there must have been a good reason for them. Helen had had her failings, intentional and deliberate cruelty hadn't been one of them.

That evening, she dressed carefully for her dinner with Nicholas. Knowing she looked her best had always given her the confidence to deal with whatever obstacle she faced. And she knew that she was facing an obstacle now of truly monumental proportions. Somehow, she had to overcome Nicholas's only too evident distrust of her and her motives for being here.

Also, he'd doubtless want to discuss her plans for the future, find out what it was she wanted to do. Maybe he was hoping that she'd accept his offer to buy her share? She knew now that she wouldn't sell to him. She wanted to stay, to find out all she could about her father for one thing. But more than that, she wanted to help run the hotel that he'd built up. It felt like the right thing to do. And Nicholas would have to accept that.

At eight o'clock precisely, she walked along the hallway to the door of the adjoining apartment. Her knock was immediately answered, almost as if he'd been awaiting her, and he unsmilingly bade her enter. Jenna felt a shiver of apprehension. His expression didn't bode well for the next hour or two. Nonetheless, this didn't stop his glance from sweeping over her.

All of this meant that she was heartily glad she'd made an effort because, surprisingly, so had he. Although, maybe he dressed for dinner each evening? She wouldn't know.

Anyway, he was attired in a tan, open necked shirt and cream trousers, and once again looked spectacularly handsome, that distinctly menacing expression that he'd worn earlier completely extinguished. 'Come in, Jenna. All settled in?'

'Yes, thank you. The apartment is fantastic. Every luxury. My father clearly had impeccable taste. I'm sure I'm going to be very happy here.'

He gave her an assessing look at that. Her words, deliberately chosen, were intended to leave him in no doubt that she meant to stay in Malta. She had resolved to start as she meant to go on and that was to hide nothing from him of her intentions concerning her future.

Nicholas said nothing, however, merely ushering her into a sitting room practically the twin of the one in which she would be spending the next years, if everything worked out as she planned.

However, where her father had furnished in an understated English style, this sitting room was most definitely Mediterranean. Pastel coloured walls, gauzy curtains at the windows that moved with the slightest breeze, cane furniture with deep, cream cushions, terracotta floor tiles throughout, brightened here and there with Chinese silk rugs, and plants, not in quite the luxuriant profusion of the reception area, but it still felt like sitting in a botanical garden.

'No parrot up here then?' she lightly asked, hoping her quip would provoke a smile upon his face, an easing of the tense atmosphere.

It didn't.

His tone and expression remained stubbornly cool. She sighed. If only she could see that smile again, the one that had initially greeted her. But she'd despatched that by lying to him. Something she now bitterly regretted. It had been stupid, short-sighted.

Her only excuse was that she'd been completely thrown by meeting him. She hadn't expected that — although, why she hadn't, she didn't really know. He was part-owner of the hotel and, as such, would be likely to be around. Still, she'd wanted to hold their first meeting at a time of her own choosing.

It was too late to do anything about it now. She'd just have to try and make the best of an uncomfortable situation.

'No, one's enough,' he said, 'the noise that Columbus makes. Please sit down.' He indicated the cane settee. 'A glass of white wine?'

'Thank you, yes.'

She noticed the table laid up on the balcony outside, identical to the one she had in her own apartment. A high bamboo partition afforded each of them their privacy.

'I thought we'd get the business over with before we eat,' he brusquely said.

'Fine by me,' she equally brusquely answered.

'I've spoken to Max Pollacco, told him you're here. He'll contact you to sort out the legal side of things. He thinks it should all be pretty straightforward.' He sipped from his glass, his suddenly darkened gaze reaching out to her over its rim, 'did Stella Delaney tell you of my wish to buy you out?'

'Yes, she did.'

'And?' His one eyebrow lifted. Jenna felt a decided sinking of her spirit. It was then that she wondered how he was going to take her refusal to sell to him? She recalled her sense of fear when he'd discovered that she'd lied about her identity and a shiver of misgiving rippled through her.

They were alone up here, after all. She eyed his powerful physique. Oh, for goodness' sake, she scolded herself, stop being so ridiculous. Nicholas Portelli wasn't going to hurt her. Yet, you did hear of single women going abroad alone and never being heard from again.

'Jenna?'

'Sorry.' She shook herself free of her morbid thoughts. There was nothing to worry about. She was in a hotel full of people; nothing was going to happen to her. 'I want to stay and help run the hotel — do whatever it was that my father did.'

'Aah.' He continued to sip his wine, his expression one of deliberation. Thankfully, the devilish look had vanished. Jenna breathed a sigh of relief. Maybe he wasn't so keen to buy her share as the solicitor had implied. 'I'm prepared to offer you a very generous sum for your 49%.'

'No, thank you,' she responded briskly. 'I want to stay. There's nothing for me in England.'

'Right.' He tilted his head to one side and studied her intently.

Jenna felt like a specimen butterfly, imprisoned on a particularly sharp pin. It wasn't a sensation she cared for. Again, a deliberate stratagem? She was beginning to think that Nicholas Portelli was an expert tactician, skilled at making his opponent feel as uncomfortable, as unsure as he could. It would undoubtedly afford him the upper hand in any dispute.

'What experience do you have in accountancy?'

The question was lobbed at her so suddenly, so unexpectedly, that it caught her totally unprepared. All she could do was stare at him, which was why she saw the expression of satisfaction cross his face. It was only fleeting, but it was there.

Her mouth tightened. He knew very well that she had no experience of accountancy. How he knew, she couldn't have said, but he knew; she'd put money on it. A lucky guess?

'Well, obviously none.' His smile then was one of supreme complacency.

Jenna gritted her teeth. She was so furious that she was sorely tempted to say yes, she did have experience in that field, simply to wipe that look from his face. But that would be a step too far. And, let's face it, he'd pretty quickly uncover her deception, proving once again that she was a liar. She wouldn't give him the satisfaction.

'Because that's what your father did,' he smoothly went on. 'He handled all the financial affairs of the hotel.' He took another mouthful of his wine.

He was hoping to intimidate her into selling to him, Jenna suddenly realised. Well, it wasn't going to work. It would take more than his arrogant assumption about her financial abilities — or lack of them, should she say, to do that. So, 'I'm a quick learner,' she shot back at him. It was now her turn to look smug. Deal with that, she mutely challenged.

'Jenna,' he sighed, as if already weary of the argument, 'the hotel business is complex enough to require the expertise of a qualified accountant and I'm quite sure that, keen to learn or not, it would take many years for you to attain that standard.'

'But haven't you been doing it since my father died?' She didn't know that, it was a stab in the dark. However, it proved a killingly accurate stab, she swiftly saw. Because his expression darkened as his brow lowered. Hah! She'd got him.

'Well, yes . . . '

Determined not to spare him, she went on, 'And are you a qualified accountant?'

'No.'

Jenna didn't quite smirk. Point number two to her. 'So —' she shrugged her shoulders, 'why can't you continue doing that and I'll take over the daily management?'

'I'll give it to you, you're a fighter.'

'I've had to be,' she smartly retaliated.

'OK, so have you had any experience of hotel management?' He was determined to beat her, and Jenna was equally determined that he shouldn't.

'Some.' It wasn't a total lie. She had helped run a small café for a couple of months, when she'd first left school. It hadn't been entirely successful which was why she'd been dismissed pretty promptly. Still, she didn't have to tell Nicholas that, and she had been telling the truth when she'd stated that she was a quick learner. She was sure she'd soon pick things up. I mean, how hard could it be to check people in, and make sure the rooms were kept clean?

'How much — exactly?' he pressed. He'd clearly picked up on her deliberate evasiveness and was now determined to pin her down.

'I helped run a restaurant.' She decided restaurant sounded better than café, and they had served meals, even if they had been mainly egg and chips or variations on that theme. There had also been another waitress working more or less beneath her, so her claim to have managed the place wasn't strictly a lie.

'Right. So no hotel experience?'

'Well, I've stayed in a few,' she quipped.

He continued to study her. There was an unnerving expression in his eye now.

It made her wonder if he'd seen straight through her shameless exaggeration?

'And then I worked in a department store, so I'm perfectly accustomed to dealing with people,' she glibly and truthfully this time assured him.

'OK.' His unexpected agreement caught her unawares. She'd been preparing herself for a great deal more argument, possibly over a period of days, maybe even weeks. His unexpected acquiescence startled her. Made her suspicious of his possible motive for this. It seemed out of character from the little she had learned about him thus far.

'It's a deal. But rather than just hand the reins over to you — after all, my interests are at stake here as well if you make a mess of things.' His tone was velvety smooth but Jenna sensed the iron resolve beneath. He wasn't about to let anyone jeopardise his 51% of this hotel. And, in all fairness, she couldn't blame him.

'So I'd like you to work with my

assistant for a while, Bernadette Dona-
tini, Bernie for short. She can show you
the ropes, and I'll be around too. If
that's OK with you, naturally?'

Oh, so he had remembered that she
was a partner, not merely an employee.
For a minute or two there, Jenna had
been convinced that he was going to
refuse to let her stay. Yet, how could he?
She did, after all, own 49% of the place.
Nonetheless, she was pretty sure that
what Nicholas Portelli wanted, he
usually got. Come what may.

Deciding that it was time to turn the
subject away from herself, before he
made the discovery that she had no
experience, whatsoever, of running
anything, let alone a hotel, she asked,
'Perhaps you could tell me how you and
my father came to be partners.'

He readily accepted her change of
subject, leading her to think that
perhaps he wasn't going to be as
difficult to work with as she'd begun to
anticipate.

'Of course. My parents also ran a

hotel, well, a couple, actually. One in Sliema and a larger one in Valletta. As I had grown up in that business, it seemed a natural thing to carry on and work in it. I helped them with theirs for some years after I left school, thereby gaining valuable experience. They became friends with your father upon his return to Malta, mainly because he stayed in the Sliema one for a short while.

'Anyway, Vince quickly decided to buy himself a hotel and for many years did very well, but then gradually it began to lose money, until in the end he needed a substantial injection of cash. Although he was an excellent accountant, he proved to be weak on the management side. A few of the staff took advantage we later discovered and hadn't pulled their weight. Customers steadily became disgruntled at the lack of service and business dropped away.

'It was then that I bought a share of the hotel, 50% to be exact. I managed the place and Vince handled the finances. It worked supremely well. Of course, eventually, as Vince became ill, I took over the financial side as well. He then gave me the extra 1%. Said it seemed only fair I have the controlling share as I was doing the bulk of the work.'

'So how old were you when you bought in?'

'Twenty-eight. That was just over seven years ago.'

'Why did my father come back here? Did he ever say?'

'Only that he came for a holiday. I don't think he had any intention of staying. He wanted to give himself some space to get over the split with your mother he later told me. Anyway, being back felt so good, he decided to stay. He said that as he got older he felt he needed the Maltese sun, rather than the English rain. He had enough money saved to part pay for the hotel. He borrowed the rest.'

'Did he talk about me?'

'All the time.' She could feel

Nicholas's gaze upon her. 'But only to me. Vince preferred to keep his private life private.'

'So, no-one else knew about me?'

'No. He once told me he regarded me as the nearest thing he had to a son. Not that I ever replaced you. No-one could have done that. He adored you.'

'But he still left me,' Jenna sadly said.

'And tried desperately to find you again, for several years. It was the deepest regret of his life that he lost contact with you.'

'And you?' For the second time, she decided to change the subject. It was distressing her too deeply to talk about her father. 'You're obviously Maltese.'

'Yes. I went to school in England, though. My parents wanted me to have an English education. My mother's grandfather was English. He married a Maltese girl so there is a drop of English blood in me. In fact, I'm named after him.'

'Are they still alive? Your parents?'

'Very much so. They live in Valletta

now. They decided they wanted to retire, so they sold both hotels and with the money they made on them bought a former Duke's palace.' He smiled for the first time that evening. Judging by the warmth of the smile, he was clearly very fond of his parents. It made him seem more human to Jenna.

After that, conversation ranged over all manner of topics. Bit by bit, Nicholas warmed and proved adept at drawing her out. He wanted to know all about her and her mother and their life together. She told him a little, briefly describing their nomadic way of living.

'It must have been hard for you, especially as you got older.' His expression told her that he thought she should have asked more questions of Helen. But why would she have? She'd trusted her mother — mistakenly, it turned out.

'It was. No time to make any real friends. Tell me,' there was one question she hadn't asked him, 'did my father ever say why he left us so suddenly?'

'No. He didn't speak about Helen much at all. I assumed it was too painful for him. I just knew he couldn't find her, and as a consequence, you. As I said, it was you he talked about. He returned to England several times when he had news of your whereabouts, but you'd always disappeared again by the time he got there. Somehow your mother must have known he'd found her.'

'I don't think she did know. She just made it a practice to keep moving. I believe she liked that lifestyle.' She wasn't about to tell him that she'd wondered if Helen had been in debt and that was why they'd moved so frequently. But something else occurred to her then. 'How did my father get news of where we were?'

'He employed a private investigator for a long time. I sometimes think that was what helped put him into such dire financial straits.'

'Oh — well, in that case, she could have known she was being watched or followed. She was a very sensitive person — almost psychic at times.'

Nicholas looked doubtful. 'I still wonder if she was afraid he'd take you away from her and that was the reason for the lies.'

His words gave Jenna hope that they could work successfully together. They had been almost an apology for his earlier suspicions of her.

'But I think he simply wanted to share in your upbringing, your growing up.'

★   ★   ★

That night, Jenna dreamed of her father. It was as if being there, in his apartment, had unleashed long buried memories. Eventually she woke, with tears upon her cheeks.

Unable to return to sleep after such a vivid and disturbing dream, she got up. She'd already found all her father's clothes in the bedroom when she'd unpacked her own things; the wardrobe had still been full, as had the chest of drawers.

A faint scent had lingered upon the garments and she'd found herself burying her face in their folds, sniffing at them, desperate for some sort of link, attachment, to the man she'd never really known. What she hadn't done was go through the bureau that sat in the corner of the sitting room. It was the most likely repository for his personal papers and correspondence.

She went there now and opened the top drawer. Everything would have to be sorted out sooner or later so she may as well make a start, she couldn't sleep, so . . .

The very first thing she saw were two letters, clipped together and addressed to her mother. She separated them and examined them. The first one was dated not that long after he'd left them. A matter of months, maybe? Not that she'd known the exact date, she'd been too young at the time. The second one had been sent some time later.

They'd both been returned — the earliest one by her mother. Jenna recognised the handwriting on the envelope: Return to sender. The other had been returned by a stranger. The words PERSON UNKNOWN AT THIS ADDRESS had been printed in an unfamiliar hand. These must be the letters that Nicholas had referred to.

Jenna's breathing quickened as the implications of this hit her. Helen had known where her husband was because the hotel's address was printed on the back of the envelope that she'd returned.

Nicholas had been right. Helen had known where Vince was. The pain stabbed at her then, as well as a deep sense of betrayal. Her mother had known perfectly well that her husband wasn't dead but had allowed her daughter to go on believing he was. It was as if her mother were here, in the room, and had physically struck her.

She went to open the earliest one but then stopped. It would feel too much like an invasion of their privacy. And it was too soon. She wasn't strong enough; not yet. Perhaps one day when she'd feel more able to cope with whatever she might read?

The truth, maybe, of exactly what had happened between her parents? Carefully, and with trembling fingers, she replaced them where she'd found them. It would be too painful at the present time — to read the words that her father had actually written.

She couldn't help wondering once again though if her mother had indeed been scared of her husband, and that was why she'd lied to her daughter for so many years? To keep her away from a man who might harm them both?

It was the only explanation that Jenna could come up with, even if it was one that she found almost impossible to contemplate, despite the fact that her dream had seemed to suggest some sort of argument. But Nicholas had described him as a gentle man. Surely, if it had been there, he'd have seen some sign of a violent streak in all their years of working together?

Jenna Finds A Friend

Having had no time to shop for groceries, the next morning Jenna decided to have breakfast in the hotel dining room. So far she'd seen very little of the place that would be her home from now on and she was eager to remedy that.

As it was early, she decided food could wait. Instead, she embarked upon a tour of the hotel, discovering various sitting rooms and bars, all done out in the pastel, Mediterranean style, as was a palatial and very elegant dining room on the second floor, its huge sliding doors standing open on to a large balcony that overlooked an even larger terrace and an Olympic-sized swimming pool.

Deciding that an inspection of what looked like extensive and professionally landscaped gardens could wait, she chose a small table in front of the open doors and sat down. She'd picked up an English newspaper from reception and had started to read that when someone walked into the back of her chair.

'Oh, skuzani — um, I mean sorry. Please, I must apologise.'

Jenna glanced up into the man's anxious face. He looked about her own age, a waiter, she guessed, mainly because he was wearing black trousers and a white shirt. Far too formal for any of the hotel's guests.

'I wasn't looking where I was going,' he explained.

'That's all right.' Jenna smiled. He was very good looking with jet black hair and hyacinth blue eyes. Although slimly built, he was tall, she guessed he would top her five feet six by a good few inches. He had the swarthy skin of the person who spent a great deal of time in the sun, and a single tantalising dimple flashed from the centre of one cheek as he smiled back at her.

'Accidents happen,' she added, by way of further reassurance. He still appeared slightly anxious, though. Was he worried that she might complain to management? To put him out of his misery, she said, 'By the way, I'm Jenna Saliba. Vincent Saliba's daughter. I've just arrived from England.'

Sadly, it did the exact opposite. He looked initially shocked and then even more anxious. 'I didn't know he had a daughter. But then why would I? I've only worked here for a couple of months.' He shrugged, his expression a strange one now as he stared at her; cool, distant.

Maybe he felt that he shouldn't be too friendly with her? With her father dead, she could quite possibly be his employer. Was that what he was thinking? Jenna felt a stab of disappointment. She would have liked to get to know him.

'Can I take your breakfast order, Ms Saliba?' he then politely asked, thus confirming her suspicion that he considered any sort of friendship between them inappropriate.

*　　*　　*

After a substantial breakfast, Jenna decided it might be sensible to walk into Mellieha. Much more food like that and in those quantities and she'd be piling on the pounds. Also, she desperately needed a few things so her lessons in learning to run the hotel could wait a day or two. There was no rush, after all. She had the rest of her life. Mellieha couldn't be more than two or three miles away, surely? Near enough to walk to and then get a taxi back.

She returned to her apartment to collect her handbag and the all-important sun hat, as it was approaching twelve o'clock and the hottest part of the day. But as she walked from the hotel and felt the heat hit her like a hammer blow, she swiftly reconsidered her decision to walk. Maybe taking a taxi both ways

83

would be the most sensible thing to do? Undecided, she stopped at the foot of the front steps, and as she did so, a motor scooter pulled up in front of her.

'Ms Saliba.' It was the young waiter.

'Hello, I don't know your name, I'm afraid.'

'It is Marc; Marc Farruq.'

'Well, hello, Marc.' She smiled encouragingly at him. She felt in desperate need of a friend, and, as things stood, at the moment he seemed the sole candidate.

'Are you going for a walk?' he asked.

'I was intending to walk into Mellieha, but . . . ' she smiled doubtfully.

'It is far too hot for such a venture and much too far to walk. I will take you.' He indicated the pillion seat, complete with helmet strapped to it. 'If you don't mind my bike, that is.' His grin was an admiring one. She basked in it, it made a welcome contrast to Nicholas Portelli's coolness.

'Well, that's very kind, but . . . '

The grin was extinguished, his earlier look of respectful distance had returned. 'Of course. Please, accept my apology.' He bowed his head remorsefully. 'It would not be proper. After all, you must be my employer now if you are Mr Saliba's daughter.'

'Oh no, that wasn't what I meant. I would love a lift, thank you.' The second the impetuous words left her lips, she wished them unsaid. Was she mad? She'd never ridden pillion on a bike in her life.

'You are my employer, I presume?' He sounded insistent. He clearly wanted to know.

'Yes, I am. Does that make a difference?'

He shrugged. 'If you don't mind, I don't. Although, what Mr Portelli would think of you doing this . . .'

She didn't give a toss what Nicholas thought. 'I don't think Mr Portelli would have any views on the matter.'

Marc raised an eyebrow at her. 'You don't?' He sounded amused. And extremely sceptical.

'No. It's up to me what I do and who I see.' In a fruitless gesture of defiance against the absent Nicholas, after all, he wasn't there to witness it, she took the crash helmet that Marc was holding out to her and strapped it on before climbing on to the bike.

Beneath a periwinkle sky, they rode along practically empty roads. Although she'd travelled this way twice before by taxi, this time Jenna seemed to see more — maybe because she was on the back of a scooter rather than sitting within the confines of a vehicle?

Stretching out to one side of them, as far as the eye could see, were the muted greens of olive trees, substantial groves of orange and lemon trees, and fields of what looked like tomato plants. On their other side was the intense blue of the sea, glittering and glistening in the sunshine, diamond-bright, inviting.

It didn't take long to reach Mellieha, despite Marc's restrained speed, where he parked outside an attractive café complete with vine shaded terrace.

'How about a drink before I leave you to your shopping? I do not have to be back at work until six o'clock.'

'I'd like that, Marc, thank you.'

Once they were seated with tall glasses of freshly squeezed orange juice in front of them, Marc studied her for a long moment, head to one side, before asking, 'And how does Nicholas Portelli feel about you being here?'

Jenna hesitated. Maybe she shouldn't discuss Nicholas with Marc? Marc was his employee — it wouldn't seem fitting.

'Are you going to stay?' Marc went on, in the absence of any response from her. 'Do what your father did? Help run the hotel? I imagine he bequeathed you his share? And that's why you are here. I take it you are an only child?'

'Yes. And yes, he did leave me his share and yes, that's why I'm here. It was originally left to my mother, but she died five years ago. The only thing is,' she hesitated. Maybe she shouldn't say anything? Nicholas might not want his plans broadcast, but she needed to talk to someone about it, and she had no intention of selling her share so there wasn't really anything for anyone to know. 'Nicholas wants to buy me out.'

'Now, why doesn't that surprise me?' His tone was one of dry cynicism. He regarded her thoughtfully. 'Did you see much of your father? I mean — if he was here and you were in England . . . '

'No, I've never been to Malta before.' She noted the flicker of surprise, and something else, something she couldn't identify, within his eyes. 'I believed him to have died twenty years ago. That's what my mother told me. Max Pollacco, my father's solicitor, instructed an English solicitor to find me.'

He frowned. 'Why would your mother have told you that?' He stopped abruptly, as if aware of crossing an invisible line. 'No, it is none of my business.'

Again, Jenna didn't respond. He was right, it was none of his business. And apart from that, it was far too early in their acquaintance for the disclosure of such private information — even had she known the answer to his question.

'So ... ' he went on, 'you didn't really know your father?'

'I didn't know him at all. He left when I was three and came straight back here, apparently.'

Marc's eyes darkened. 'I did not know my father either. He deserted my mother months before I was born.' His face hardened into harshly sculpted planes and his eyes turned into chips of ice. 'So, we have a great deal in common, you and I, Ms Saliba. Maybe we can be friends?'

'I hope so, and please call me Jenna. I don't know anyone here yet — apart from Nicholas, of course, and I can hardly describe him as a friend,' she dryly added, 'so I'll be glad of your company.' Even if he was several years younger than her she'd realised upon closer inspection, eighteen or nineteen at the most, and extremely inquisitive.

'As I will be yours, Jenna.' His expression had lightened once more and his eyes warmed. 'But just a word of warning. Be careful of Nicholas Portelli. He is a very determined man, ruthless one might almost say. And if he wants your share of the hotel, well, all I'm saying is — watch your back. Mr Portelli is accustomed to getting everything that he desires.'

Marc's words left an unpleasant aftertaste with Jenna, but when she pressed him to elaborate on this statement he refused to say any more.

Which meant that she was so preoccupied with his admonition, and whatever it was he hadn't wanted to disclose, that she ended up returning to the hotel without one half of what she needed.

Oh, stop it, she eventually told herself, as her brooding thoughts grew darker and darker, Marc must have been exaggerating. Still, she couldn't forget the fleeting sense of being threatened that she had experienced in Nicholas's company — which made Marc's warning suddenly seem not quite so ridiculous.

In a bid to distract herself from her disturbing reflections, she decided she'd walk to the secluded bay that a guide book which she'd picked up first thing that morning along with the newspaper had referred to. She'd asked Marc about it, saying, 'I thought I'd go this afternoon.'

'Good idea. It is nice there. Out of the way. Never gets too crowded.'

For a second, she expected him to add, 'I'll come with you,' he had the rest of the day off, and it would have been pleasant to have his company. But he didn't. Maybe he'd thought better of it?

Instead, he said, 'Well, Jenna, have a nice day,' before standing and going on, 'I'll maybe see you later,' and he was quickly gone, leaving Jenna with an unexpected sense of abandonment.

It was as she was crossing the reception area that she saw Nicholas. A shiver of apprehension rippled through her. She mustn't allow Marc's words to influence her with regards to Nicholas. She must get to know him, overcome her misgivings about him and his intentions towards her.

She couldn't imagine him wishing to harm her; not when he'd been so close to her father. And not even if he wanted to own the hotel outright.

He spotted her and strode across to her, his step confident; self-assured.

'How are you?' he asked.

'Fine. I was thinking, I'd like to see my father's grave.'

'Aah, bit difficult that. Vince was cremated. His wish . . . '

'Oh, I see.' She hadn't considered that possibility. 'Well, where are his ashes?'

'Scattered in his favourite part of the garden. The rose walk. That's what he wanted. We've placed a small memorial plaque there.'

'Thank you. I'll go and have a look this evening when it's quieter. Less people around.'

'Would you like me to show you?'

'No, thank you. I'm sure I'll be able to find it.' She wanted to be alone when she went. To feel closer to her father. She also had a strong suspicion that she'd weep and she didn't want a witness — any witness to that.

'When did you plan to start working?'

His gaze rested, disapprovingly she felt, upon her beach bag. Although, why he should disapprove of her going out for a while she couldn't imagine. And it was none of his business what she did.

Nonetheless, it was in a slightly embarrassed tone that she said, 'I was going to have a word with you about that. I thought that I'd have a few days holiday first. You know, see a bit of Malta . . . '

'Of course. You must do whatever you wish to. I don't intend to be a hard task master.'

You won't be a task master at all, was Jenna's unspoken response to that. I'm a partner, not an employee. Maybe she should remind him of that. That she was Vince's daughter . . .

'But if you wish to learn all there is to know, and there's rather a lot, I shouldn't leave it too long to begin.'

So, he'd obviously been referring to him training her in hotel management. Thank heavens she hadn't remonstrated with him. She'd have felt pretty silly now.

'Where are you off to? Somewhere nice? I could probably suggest a few places to go.'

'I thought the beach around the corner.'

'Aah, Mursaloq Lagoon — well, it's not really a lagoon, just a bay that's partially enclosed by twin headlands.'

'Yes, that's what the guidebook said.'

'OK, well, enjoy yourself. Be careful of the sun, it's very strong at this time of year, and you're quite fair skinned.' His gaze roamed over her, lingering momentarily on her exposed skin.

* ★ *

Jenna stood on the cliff top and looked down at the small beach way below her. She had no head for heights and the flight of wooden steps which ran down the sheer cliff face, and which she would have to negotiate to join the other people on the beach, looked green with age and positively dangerous.

There was no other way down, however, which meant that everyone there had managed to descend safely. Why should she be any less capable? Telling herself not to be such a pathetic wimp, and, trying very hard to disregard a stomach that was churning with terror, she grabbed the hand rail and started to descend.

Very slowly, she lowered her foot to the first step — and then, gingerly, to the second. Nothing shook, the steps didn't, as she'd feared, collapse beneath her; the structure was perfectly sound. She took a deep breath. See, she told herself, there's nothing to worry about. Her descent quickened as her confidence grew.

She was almost halfway down when something large and heavy struck her in the middle of her back, propelling her forward, wrenching her hand off the railing, and making her miss her footing. And all of a sudden, she was falling, head first and directly towards the rocks that lay below. If she hit those, was all she had time to think, she'd break her neck and it would all be over.

Desperate to save herself, she let go of her bag and by twisting herself sideways and flinging out an arm, somehow managed to grab hold of the railing again, thereby halting her headlong descent. She hadn't, however, managed to prevent her bumpy fall down several of the steps, her side and ribs taking the full impact of her tumble.

She lay across the steps, right where she'd landed, her one hand still tightly gripping the rail as she struggled to quell the feeling of nausea that was threatening to overwhelm her. It was a full two or three minutes before she managed to sit upright, and, even then, she continued to shake. She swivelled her head to look back up the steps to where she'd been when she started falling.

Something had struck her, but she could see nothing that could have caused her to lose balance. She looked down, and it was then that she noticed a large stone — well, a small boulder, really — lying to one side of the much larger rocks at the foot of the steps. Could that have been what hit her? If it had been, where had it come from?

'Are you all right?'

It was a man, English by the sound of it. 'I saw you fall.' He hurried up the steps to her and helped her to her feet. He was holding her bag. 'OK?' he asked again. 'Do you speak English?'

'Yes. I-I am English,' she haltingly told him. 'I think I'm OK, thank you.

My side hurts but apart from that . . . '
Gingerly, she moved her limbs, her shoulder . . . 'Ouch! That's painful. But I think it's only bruising.' Her ribs felt really tender. Could she have broken them?

'I saw a boulder hurtling down,' he told her, 'and I thought I saw someone standing at the top of the steps.'

Jenna stared at him, horrified. 'What?' She looked back up to the top of the cliff. No-one was there. She turned back to the man. 'You saw someone?'

'Yes — well, I think so.' His brow wrinkled.

'Could whoever it was have thrown the boulder?' She didn't want to think such a thing, but after Marc's warning words about Nicholas, she couldn't help herself. It was now the stranger's turn to look horrified. She speedily changed tack. She didn't want to start a rumour about some mad person knocking people off of steps. 'Or maybe dislodged it with a foot?'

The man's expression cleared. 'Couldn't say.'

'Was it a man or a woman?'

Helplessly, he shook his head. 'Sorry. I'm not much use, am I? But the truth is I couldn't see clearly enough. And whoever it was was gone in a flash. In fact,' he admitted now, somewhat sheepishly, 'I could have made a mistake, I suppose, and just thought I saw someone. My eyesight's not what it was and the sun is terribly bright, casting shadows everywhere.'

'Is She In Danger?'

Not surprisingly, after that Jenna lost the urge to lie on a beach, and instead limped back to the hotel. Clearly no bones were broken because she could move, but she expected to find plenty of bruises when she looked.

She didn't know what to believe. Could someone have been at the top of the steps? Someone who could have hurled the rock at her back? Their intention to unbalance her? To make her fall? If that had indeed been the case, then their plan had almost worked. For, if she had gone all the way down, head first, and landed on the rocks below, she would almost certainly have been killed.

There was only one person she could think of who might want rid of her that badly. Nicholas. She'd already felt threatened by him. And he'd know where she was headed, because she'd told him. Her demise, bearing in mind the terms of her father's will, could very well work to his advantage.

If she'd been deceased, as well as her mother, then her share of the hotel would have gone to Nicholas, thus giving him the 100% he seemed to want. Which begged the question — if she should die now, with no descendants of her own, would he still get her share? And then there was Marc's warning to be taken into account. Be careful of Nicholas Portelli. Watch your back, he'd told her. But he couldn't have meant that literally. He couldn't possibly have foreseen her accident, could he?

No, no matter how much Nicholas might want her share of the hotel, she simply couldn't believe him capable of murder. Didn't want to believe him capable of such a thing.

Still, maybe, as a precaution, she ought to make her will, and then, somehow, let him know that someone else would inherit in the event of her death? But who could she leave her share to? Pauline? If Nicholas was indeed out to get rid of her, wouldn't she just be putting Pauline in danger?

If she truly believed Nicholas capable of such a wicked act, then how could she stay here? Her life could be in danger. Yet, the man who'd come to her aid hadn't been at all sure of what he'd seen, or even if he had actually seen anything.

If someone had indeed been there, it had very probably been an innocent passer-by. Someone who had stopped to admire the view and had accidentally dislodged the rock. That had to be the explanation.

But if it was, why hadn't they waited to make sure that she was all right? They must have seen what happened.

Needing some sort of distraction from these disturbing questions and their equally disturbing answers, despite her aching ribs and side, Jenna decided to go and look for the rose walk. She guessed all the guests would be either relaxing by the pool or out somewhere sightseeing at this time of the afternoon, thus affording her the privacy she desired.

★ ★ ★

It didn't take her long to find it and she was gratified to discover it deserted. The air was heady with the scent of dozens of rose bushes, as well as filled with the choir-like hum of the cicadas. Conscious of any potential bruising she took her time walking the pathway through them, gingerly bending to sniff at the occasional bloom, all the time her gaze searching for the memorial plaque that Nicholas had assured her was here.

She eventually spotted it, almost buried beneath a particularly fragrant bush. She moved some of the thorny branches to one side to give a clearer view, tearing her fingers in the process, and then stood, absent-mindedly sucking the blood away, looking down at it for several moments.

Just as she'd expected, it didn't take long for tears to start stinging her eyes and the few memories she had to come flooding back. Of a father who had loved her very much, just as Nicholas had said. As young as she'd been, she did remember that. So why had he abandoned her?

* * *

Come the next morning, after a practically sleepless night, mainly due to the dull ache in her side, ribs and shoulder where they'd struck the steps, she decided to forego the few days of holiday she'd promised herself and get down to learning all she could about the hotel business. She had a lot of ground to cover and the sooner she started the better. It would also take her mind off what had so nearly happened the day before and the many questions that the accident had provoked.

She showered and put on what she

considered suitable wear for a day's work: a cream, sleeveless blouse and a mint green, knee-length skirt. She topped it with a lightweight, cream jacket.

She then swallowed a couple of the painkillers she'd discovered in the bathroom cabinet and went to what she presumed would be her and Nicholas's office. She'd noticed the two desks in there on her first visit, so she guessed one had been her father's.

She thought she detected the faintest glimmer of amusement upon Nicholas's face as she took her seat at the vacant desk. Had she dressed too formally? From Nicholas's expression, he clearly thought so. He was clad in an open necked shirt and cotton trousers. 'Well, that was a brief holiday. From the look of you, you're here to work.'

'Yes, I thought I'd get started. Lots to learn.' She debated telling him about yesterday's incident, just to see how he reacted, but almost at once thought better of it. Her side and ribs remained sore, as did her shoulder. Not surprising, really.

As she'd expected, she was quite badly bruised. In spite of the painkillers, she suspected she'd need to be cautious about how she moved, but it was nothing she couldn't cope with.

She felt rather silly, truth to tell, going out for the first time and managing to fall down a flight of steps that everyone else lying on the beach below had managed to successfully negotiate.

She'd firmly discounted the suspicion that someone had deliberately heaved the rock at her. It had to have been an accident. Any other possibility was totally unacceptable.

'Right. Good. So — you plan to take over the day to day running of the hotel — is that right?'

'Well, eventually, yes. Obviously I'll need to learn a few things first.'

'Just a few — yes.'

Was that another jibe at her confidence in her ability to help run the hotel? If it was, he clearly expected her to fail. Well, if that were the case, he was going to have to revise that expectation. Because she was going to prove him, and anyone else who doubted her ability, wrong.

Jenna tightened her lips, and said nothing — much as she was tempted to bite back. She refused to give him the satisfaction of knowing he'd got to her. 'You said I could work with your assistant.'

'Bernie, yes. She'll take you under your wing. I've already mentioned it to her. Come on. I'll introduce you.'

And he stood up and strode from the office. Jenna speedily followed, trying to disregard the pain that had been induced. He didn't believe in wasting time, did he? Was he always like this? A powerhouse of energy? If so, she was going to have considerable trouble keeping up — for a day or two, at any rate.

Bernie turned out to be an attractive, sophisticated woman, Jenna guessed in her early forties, smartly dressed, which lessened Jenna's feeling of being a bit OTT, and oozing self-confidence. Just like her boss, Jenna mused. Hopefully, some of it would rub off on her. She was certainly in need of it at the present time.

'Bernie,' Nicholas hailed her, the warmth of his greeting a marked contrast to his manner whenever he was with Jenna. A miniscule pang of hurt made itself felt in her chest; she instantly banished it. What did she care what Nicholas Portelli thought of her. As long as she got to stay here — that was all that mattered, and Nicholas would have to learn to live with that. 'I've brought you your trainee. This is Jenna, Vince's daughter.'

Bernie's gaze sharpened with interest. 'Nice to meet you, Jenna. I'm sure we'll work well together.'

'Jenna wants to learn to manage the hotel on a day to day basis, Bernie, as I explained. So, what's the best way to do that?'

'Well, ideally to have a go at each of the jobs involved,' Bernie replied. 'Get a feel for them so you'll understand the problems as they arise and be able to sort them out.'

'Sounds good,' Jenna agreed. 'Where should I start?'

'How about the kitchen? And then a spot of waitressing. You'll get to know the staff and how they work.'

Jenna struggled to hide the dismay she felt at being assigned the lowliest of jobs; she suspected she didn't quite succeed — if Nicholas's expression was anything to go by.

She wasn't surprised. She'd always been hopeless at concealing her emotions. Her mother used to say, 'Jenna, don't ever try to play poker. You'll lose a fortune.'

So, all she said was, 'OK,' whilst silently conceding that it would undoubtedly be the best way to learn. From the very bottom. At least Bernie hadn't suggested cleaning the rooms. Although, she supposed that could come at a later date?

'Right. So would you like to follow me?'

'I'll leave you both to it then,' Nicholas said.

Although his tone was perfectly even, this time Jenna definitely detected amusement in his eyes. He was enjoying this. Could that be his intention — in collusion with Bernie, obviously? To discourage her from staying by giving her all the lowliest of jobs? It would seem a much more likely possibility than trying to harm her.

She let out her breath slowly. If that was his intention, she'd soon show him; show them both — that she wasn't about to be defeated so easily. That it would take more than a spell in the kitchen to despatch her back to England, tail between her legs.

However, by the end of the day, she was no longer quite so sure of that. She'd been on her feet for hours. The beneficial effect of the painkillers had long worn off — too late, she realised she should have brought more with her. There'd been none to be had in the kitchen, something she'd remedy tomorrow. There should be a supply in case any of the staff ever needed them.

So between the pain and the rigours of the job, she felt totally relaxed. Not that she wasn't accustomed to standing around, her job at the department store had entailed a great deal of that. But here, in the hotel, she wasn't just standing around, she was also running here, there and everywhere, collecting dirty dishes and pans and washing them — she'd talk to Nicholas about getting another dishwasher, one wasn't sufficient — fetching vegetables in sacks and boxes and then peeling and chopping them. Washing the kitchen floor time and time again when things got spilt.

Eventually though, she finished and dragged herself up to her apartment, where she collapsed into a hot bath. The bruises were really starting to come out. It was a wonder she'd managed to do as much as she had that day. Mind you, she silently admitted, once or twice she'd been on the verge of conceding defeat and abandoning the whole idea of staying here on Malta. But, once again, had come a resolve, a determination to show Nicholas that she would not be beaten, however laborious and tedious the tasks which he and Bernie set her, and so, she'd soldiered on.

She'd just climbed back out of the water, and wrapped a large bath towel around herself, when there was a knock on her apartment door. She opened it just a couple of inches to find Nicholas standing there.

Instinctively, she clutched the towel more tightly, and, for modesty's sake, made sure she remained hidden by the door. Of all people to catch her at such a moment, it had to be him. Although, who she'd expected it to be she couldn't have said.

'Sorry,' he clearly wasn't, judging by the glint in his eye, 'to disturb you. I was wondering how today went?'

'Oh, fine,' she said sarcastically, quite forgetting she'd intended keeping the door partially closed and instead let it swing open. 'I know all there is to know about washing dishes and scouring pans.'

Securing the towel firmly around her by the simple method of jamming both her elbows against it, she started to tick off each task on her fingers. 'As well as things like peeling potatoes, chopping tomatoes and onions. Oh, and let's not forget the extremely skilled job of washing the floor several times over.' Her eyes spat her indignation at him. 'Of course, I knew very little about any of that.'

His gaze narrowed, whether in amusement or anger at her sarcasm, she couldn't have said. Not that she cared either way by this time. 'But then, you must have started with the basics too, I'm quite sure.'

'Well,' he said, the merest quiver in his voice, 'I have to admit I didn't actually begin in the kitchen.'

'Oh,' she cried, 'did you not?' Now why didn't that surprise her?

'No, and I should think a day in there was more than enough for you too.'

'Quite,' she bit back, 'I mean how much more do I need to learn about food preparation and washing dishes?'

His lips definitely twitched now as the gleam in his eye intensified. Just like the evening before, he was beginning to appear human, rather than the devil in man's clothing that he'd initially seemed to be. 'Well, in that case, I imagine a stint on the reception desk would suit you rather better. That will teach you more about hotel management, sorting out the day to day problems as and when they arise, wouldn't you agree?'

'I would.'

'Good. Well, do that tomorrow. I've already spoken to Bernie and she agrees. We'll expect you by eight o'clock.'

'Fine. I'll be there.'

'Um . . . ' he indicated her shoulder, it was the first time he'd allowed his glance to drop to her towel draped body ' . . . that's a nasty bruise. What happened?'

Jenna instinctively lifted a hand to cover it. Maybe she should mention her fall and see how he reacted? If he reacted with nothing more than surprised concern, it would prove he hadn't been behind it and would set her mind at rest. But if he showed no surprise, what then? In the light of that question, she contented herself with simply saying, 'Oh that. I knocked it in the kitchen. It's nothing.'

'Hmm,' he regarded her thoughtfully, 'well, be careful. We don't want you bruised and battered on the reception desk, do we? People might think we're not treating you well.'

*　*　*

From then on, Jenna spent all of her time in reception. She got to know the staff and the way they worked. She could also move easily from there to wherever she was needed, the restaurant, the kitchen, deal with the cleaning staff and all matters of hotel housekeeping. She swiftly filled two notebooks with all that she was learning, which proved an invaluable source of reference.

But what she enjoyed most of all was talking to the guests and sorting out their queries and complaints. She very quickly compiled a list of reliable repair firms: electricians, plumbers, general handymen for anything she couldn't deal with herself. She worked alongside Bella on the desk, the pretty dark-haired, dark-eyed receptionist that she'd met upon her visit to confess to Nicholas that she was Vince's daughter.

Marc also made a point of calling to speak to her several times a day. On the fourth day, he invited her for a drink that evening.

At least someone was interested in her progress, she reflected, somewhat bitterly, because apart from two or three fleeting glimpses as he went about his business, she'd seen nothing at all of Nicholas. Just when he'd started to appear more human; warmer.

She'd expected him to monitor her performance a little more closely, seeing as how she was his partner. She wondered now if he'd been equally as distant from her father? It would explain why he could tell her so little about Vince's personal life.

'I'd love to, Marc,' she now said.

'Good. I will see you down here at eight o'clock.' And, with a smile, he was gone.

Bella glanced at her speculatively. 'He seems keen.'

'Does he?' Jenna deliberately spoke absently. 'I think he's just being friendly. He's a bit young for me.'

'Ye-es, I wondered about that. He is only just nineteen.'

'He told me. He also said he never knew his father.'

'Yes, I heard the same. Have you met his mother?'

'No. Have you?' Curiosity flared within Jenna. That and sympathy for a woman deserted so callously by the father of her unborn child.

'Yes. She worked here, briefly, before Marc was born. I haven't seen much of her since. Marc's only been here for a couple of months. He didn't really know your father. He was ill by that time so didn't have anything to do with the running of the hotel.'

'You were here then, when Marc's mother worked here?' Jenna was surprised. Bella didn't look old enough to have been here that long.

'Yes. I've worked here for over twenty years, with a couple of breaks to have my children. Your father was a good employer once he took over. Kind, understanding.' Bella eyed her, her expression one of speculation. 'You must have missed him when he left.'

'Yes.'

'We were all very surprised to know he had a daughter. You couldn't have been very old when he left.'

'I was three. I don't remember much about him at all. Um, could you ring the plumber? There's a problem with the shower in room 106.' She really didn't wish to discuss her father, not at the moment. And certainly not here, in public view on the reception desk.

★   ★   ★

At eight o'clock precisely, Jenna descended to the reception hall to find Marc waiting. 'Wow! You look gorgeous,' he enthused. 'I'll have every other man madly jealous of my luck,' and he grinned engagingly at her. Columbus's exuberant wolf whistle confirmed the compliment.

'Thank you,' Jenna replied. She hadn't been sure what to wear, uncertain about where Mark could be taking her. She couldn't imagine him dressing formally so she'd opted for a pair of cream linen, cropped trousers and a pretty lacy top.

'I thought I'd better not subject you

to the thrills of riding my bike this evening, so I've ordered a taxi,' he told her with a glint of mischief.

'Phew! That's a relief.' And she pretended to mop her brow.

'Going out?'

Jenna whirled. It was Nicholas. Where had he appeared from? After his marked absence on the scene over the past days, she'd begun to wonder if he were deliberately avoiding her. Although why he should do that, she couldn't imagine.

'Yes,' she said, 'Marc's very kindly asked me out for a drink.'

Nicholas's glance at the young man was a strange one. In fact, Jenna would have said he wasn't best pleased by what she'd just told him. 'You're not riding on that death trap of a bike, I trust.' His voice was tart and his mouth had tightened into a thin line of disapproval.

'No,' Jenna hastily said, 'Marc's ordered a taxi.'

'Good. Um — ' he glanced back at

Jenna again, his expression scarcely less disapproving than when he'd looked at Marc, 'we'll have a chat tomorrow, at lunchtime. Meet me on the balcony outside the dining room at one. We'll eat together.'

Jenna bristled. What had happened to the more human side he'd begun to exhibit? She wondered though whether she'd done something wrong? 'About anything specific?' she ventured to ask.

'Your progress to date.'

'Right. One o'clock it is then.' She was as business-like as he had been.

'Fine. Have a good evening then.' Something in his expression, however, told Jenna that he didn't mean that at all.

★ ★ ★

The evening passed pleasantly enough but the difference in their ages, although not great, swiftly proved significant enough for Jenna and Marc's conversation to become stilted and forced. Eventually, in desperation, Jenna asked, 'Tell me about your mother. I believe she worked at the hotel before you were born.'

'Who told you that?' His eyes narrowed and his words were sharp.

'Um, Bella. Shouldn't she have?'

He shrugged but didn't answer her question. 'Yes, she did work there briefly. She was forced to give it up when she was pregnant with me. She wasn't well so she went and stayed with her sister on the other side of the island. We didn't return here until I was, oh, let me think, two I believe.'

'And she brought you up on her own?'

'Yes, well . . . ' he snorted, 'my father certainly wasn't around to help.' His tone conveyed his utter contempt for the man who'd been so markedly absent in his life. 'Enough about me. Have another drink?'

Just like her with Bella earlier, he clearly didn't want to discuss his father, so she readily changed the subject and soon found herself rashly telling him about her fall on the cliff steps.

Marc was horrified. 'You could have been seriously hurt or even killed.'

'I know. But I wasn't, so . . . '

'Tell me exactly what happened. How the rock managed to hit you.'

'Well, a man who was there and saw me fall said he thought he'd seen someone standing at the top of the steps just before.'

'What! Could whoever it was have heaved the rock?' Marc's alarm was such that she instantly regretted telling him what had happened. 'Did he see who it was?'

'No. In fact, he wasn't even sure he'd actually seen anyone there, or whether it was just the sun casting shadows.' She grimaced ruefully. 'And as for what caused the rock to drop?' She shrugged. 'Maybe whoever it was loosened it with a foot, dislodged it, it fell, and they scarpered. That was my theory anyway. Either that or it was loose and simply broke away.'

'And drop with enough force to topple you. Unlikely. No, it was Nicholas.'

'Don't be ridiculous. Why would it be Nicholas?' She wasn't about to say that she'd had the very same thought in the beginning.

'Because if you'd been seriously injured or even killed, it would rid him of you, which means the hotel could well end up his — totally. It's what he wants, that's obvious. Look at how he is with you. Cold, critical, domineering. No-one would think you are his partner the way he speaks to you. And a convenient fall — well, it could all be put down to an accident.' He spoke with an angry bitterness.

'I can't believe that Nicholas Portelli would be capable of . . . '

'What would have happened to your father's share of the hotel if you'd — ' he paused, as if reluctant to go on, 'I don't like to mention such a thing, but what would have happened if you'd also been dead?' He smiled apologetically.

'It would have gone to Nicholas, but that doesn't mean . . . '

But Marc had fallen silent, his gaze a thoughtful one; sorrowful, even. 'In that case, Jenna, there's something I think you should know.' He paused again, as if loath to continue. 'In fact, I'm surprised nobody's mentioned it to you already.'

'What? Mentioned what, Marc?' A feeling of dread was creeping over Jenna.

'Did you know that Nicholas was once married?'

'Married! No, I didn't.' The dread was superseded by a sense of shock. Why had no-one mentioned it? Why hadn't Nicholas mentioned it, come to that? It was the sort of thing one would tell the person they were going to work with, or was it? Maybe Nicholas was every bit as private a man as her father had been? I mean, she hadn't told Nicholas all about her personal affairs.

'No, I imagine that he prefers to forget he ever was.' Marc spoke disparagingly. He clearly had very little time, or respect, for Nicholas. Jenna felt uneasy about that. After all, he'd known Nicholas longer than she had, so he must have good reason for feeling that way.

'He married Vanessa Cellini, the only child of two fairly rich people. He was twenty-two when they married, she was nineteen. They bought a house just outside Valletta. Anyway, to cut a long story short, her parents were killed in a boating accident four years after and she inherited everything, a sum, so I heard, of somewhere in the region of half a million.

'A year later Vanessa conveniently had an accident at the very same set of steps where you fell. But whereas you survived, she didn't. She'd broken her neck in the fall and died instantly. Nicholas, of course, inherited all of her money — just at the right time, apparently, to buy into your father's hotel.'

'What are you saying, Marc?' The

dread was converted into horror. A horror of what Marc was about to say next.

'What I am saying is, Nicholas was suspected of having a hand in her fall. There was a police investigation but nothing could be proved against him and he got away with it. Like your accident, someone had been seen at the top of the steps a few moments before she fell — a man. The only difference was the witness was positive that someone had been there. The police thought, given the money he stood to inherit, that it could have been Nicholas Portelli.

'He denied ever having been there, naturally, and no-one could prove otherwise, although he hadn't been able to provide a satisfactory alibi. They never did discover who the man was at the top of the steps. The police appealed for him to come forward but he never did and eventually the case was closed. The final verdict was accidental death.'

'But it doesn't mean it was Nicholas. It could have been anyone. Or, if the steps had been wet, slippery, she could just have slipped and fell.'

'So why didn't whoever it was come forward? Tell the police that? They must have seen her fall.'

'Afraid of being blamed for the fall?' She'd wondered the same thing right after her own fall. 'Maybe they too had somehow dislodged a rock?'

'There was no suggestion of that at the time. No sign of a fallen rock. I suppose it is remotely possible she missed her footing. Personally, I suspect he pushed her.'

'How do you know all this? You could only have been a child at the time.'

'That didn't prevent me from hearing the gossip. It was the talk of the island.'

* * *

A taxi deposited them both back at the hotel at the end of the evening. Marc insisted on seeing her to her door. 'I want to make sure you get inside in one piece,' he said.

He formally shook her by the hand and then left. The perfect gentleman. She smiled ruefully. Pity he was so young.

She'd just started to undress when a knock sounded on her door. She shrugged her top back on. Had Marc changed his mind?

'Marc? Oh . . . '

It wasn't Marc; it was Nicholas.

'Sorry to disappoint you.'

'You haven't.'

'Can I come in?'

'Of course.' Despite her consent, a tingle of fear edged along her spine. Marc's tale of Vanessa echoed again in her head, shaking her conviction that the instigator of her fall couldn't have been Nicholas. Nonetheless, she stood to one side to allow him entry. He'd think it strange if she didn't.

'I wanted a quick word. I really don't think it's appropriate for you to be seeing a member of staff, a younger member of staff at that, on a social basis. It gives quite the wrong impression.'

Jenna was speechless. The sheer arrogance of the man, telling her what she should and shouldn't be doing. Well he was obviously reverting to type. The gentler side he'd begun to occasionally reveal must have been some sort of aberration. But why couldn't he have said this tomorrow at lunch?

'You do realise he's only . . . '

She dragged her thoughts away from several very disturbing images of her own violent demise. 'Nineteen. Yes, I do. And I think it's my own affair who I see.'

'Not the most sensible use of a word.'

'What?' She blinked at him, puzzled.

'Affair?'

'Oh.' The impact of what he'd said struck her then. 'Oh no. It's nothing like that. What do you take me for?'

'As your partner, I consider it very much my business, too. You can't issue orders by day and then flirt by night with the same man. It undermines any authority.'

'I haven't been flirting. It's not like that. At least Marc has bothered to keep in touch with me — make sure I'm OK. Be a friend,' she finished angrily.

'Oh, I see,' he drawled, that exasperating eyebrow rising once again. 'You want a friend. Because you're feeling neglected? I haven't hovered around sufficiently, is that it? Haven't kept in close enough contact? Well, let me rectify that immediately. Is this close enough for you?'

And reaching out, he grabbed her by the shoulders, to yank her towards him. Jenna had no time to react in any way, other than to feel a veritable explosion of fear. But in the next second, his head had lowered to hers and, unbelievably, instead of trying to hurt her, he was kissing her.

A Voice From The Past

Jenna froze. She couldn't believe this was happening. That Nicholas was actually kissing her. She also couldn't believe the sheer strength of her response, as, for a single crazy moment she returned his kiss.

Good grief! What on earth was she doing? Kissing a man she couldn't be sure didn't wish her harm; hadn't already tried to harm her. A man, moreover, whom she barely knew and who, once again, was treating her with barely veiled contempt.

She wrenched herself free, lifting a hand that wasn't quite steady to her trembling lips. 'Wh-what do you think you're doing?'

He gave a snort of laughter. 'I'd have thought that was self-evident. Sorry. I shouldn't have done that. It was uncalled for.' And, indeed, he did look repentant. 'Jenna . . . ' He stretched out a hand to her.

But Jenna had had more than enough for one evening. She ignored it. 'I'll see you for lunch tomorrow, Nicholas,' and she went to the door, flinging it open in a gesture that made it more than clear that she wished him to leave. The second he'd done so, and without another word passing between them, she vigorously slammed it shut.

But once she was alone again, she lay, unable to sleep. One question, and one question only, repeated itself endlessly in her head. Why had he kissed her? Up till now he'd exhibited no sign of attraction to her. No evidence of desire. In fact, his manner towards her had suggested the exact opposite. So why?

Almost at once, a possible answer presented itself. He could be trying to win her over to persuade her to sell her share of the hotel to him.

Yet, despite what Marc had told her, and what she herself had just hazarded a guess at — she simply couldn't believe Nicholas capable of murder. Or stupid enough to try, come to that. For whatever else she might think of him, she was beginning to recognise the fact that Nicholas Portelli was an extremely astute man. And he'd been suspected of exactly the same thing once before and in exactly the same place.

If it happened a second time, old suspicions, accusations, would almost certainly be resurrected, and then examined even more closely. He must know that. And yet, on at least two occasions, he had appeared threatening. And he clearly liked to have his own way. But, she asked herself, would that be sufficient motive for cold-blooded murder?

She sighed and, closing her eyes, made a concerted effort to sleep. She was going nowhere, rehashing events — other than into another dead end.

But something even more disturbing happened the next day.

★   ★   ★

She met Nicholas for lunch as they'd arranged. She'd prepared herself for a second amorous advance by him and, despite her doubts about him and his intentions towards her, couldn't help feeling disappointed when he didn't make one.

In fact, he made no reference at all to the kiss that they'd shared the night before, not that she'd expected him to. But the fact that he'd patently dismissed it as irrelevant and forgotten about it felt almost insulting.

'I hear you're coming on very well, sorting out problems on your own, taking the initiative,' he said, leading Jenna to wonder who it was who'd been reporting her progress to him? Bella? She seemed the most likely candidate. 'Maybe you could take on more duties, start managing everything on a proper basis? How would you feel about that?'

Rapturously happy, Jenna felt like yelling. However, that might be a bit over the top, so she contented herself with saying, 'I'd like that. I'm enjoying the work. It's so varied.'

'So — no change of mind about selling your share to me?'

Jenna stared at him, struggling to interpret his expression. Was he angry about that or resigned to her staying here? She couldn't tell. Heavy lids effectively cloaked whatever emotion he might be experiencing. 'No, I want to stay. I am half Maltese, after all, due to having a Maltese father, so it could legitimately be said I've returned home — as my father did.' Her voice trembled slightly.

By declaring her intention to remain, would she be inviting another attempt on her life? If that was indeed what the incident at the beach had been. It was a terrifying prospect.

'OK. Well, it means less work for me.' He spoke lightly, as if her staying meant little or nothing to him. Jenna didn't know whether to be relieved by that or, for the second time, insulted.

★ ★ ★

It was past three o'clock by the time they eventually parted. The dining room was empty, tables cleared and waiting to be laid again for dinner that evening.

'I think I'll take a walk around the garden,' Jenna said to him before they parted. 'After that lunch, I need some exercise — if that's OK with you, of course?'

Nicholas merely inclined his head and then stood and watched her go, his expression one of deep reflection. Her subtle sarcasm hadn't been lost on him.

Jenna ran lightly down the stairs from the dining room and walked on to the terrace from beneath the balcony. She stopped and for several minutes watched a group of children playing boisterously and extremely noisily in the pool. Which was probably why she didn't see, or even hear, the scraping of one of the large stone, plant-filled pots as it started to topple from the balcony above.

It took a man's warning shout to

alert her. 'Look out! Move!' And just a split second later, as she leapt out of the way, it fell and shattered on the paving stones, precisely where she had been standing, missing her by mere inches.

'Are you all right?' The man who'd shouted ran to her. 'It's Ms Saliba, isn't it? That was a near thing.'

It was one of the hotel guests.

'Mr Blake.' She knew him by name because he'd complained about a faulty lamp in his room just the day before. 'Thank heavens you saw . . . ' She had begun to shake as the full implications of what had happened struck her.

'Someone should check those pots up there,' he angrily said. 'For one to fall off like that. How on earth could it have happened?'

'I-I don't know.' But she was beginning to entertain an awful suspicion. A second unfortunate incident? Or a second attempt to kill her? And right after she'd confirmed to Nicholas that she was staying. She'd even told him she was going to have a walk. He could easily have watched from the balcony, and then, seeing her standing right below, have pushed the pot through the gap in the balustrade.

There had been no-one left in the dining room, no-one to see him pushing and then tilting it sufficiently for it to fall. She wrapped her arms about herself, desperately trying the halt the shudders of horror that were now afflicting her. And suddenly, there were people approaching from all sides, one of whom was Marc.

'Jenna,' he gasped, obviously out of breath from the exertion of running to her side, 'are you OK? I saw what happened from inside. Did he hurt you?'

The man with Jenna looked confused, then, almost immediately, outraged. 'I haven't done anything. It was me who shouted.'

'Not you,' Marc snapped.

'Marc . . . ' Jenny spoke warningly. 'No-one has tried to hurt me. The pot fell . . . '

'Yes, but how?'

'I-I don't know.'

'Jenna, what's happened?'

This time it was Nicholas, pushing his way through the small crowd of people who had gathered.

One woman said, 'That pot fell off the balcony. It's disgraceful. Someone could have been killed. What if a child had been standing beneath?

'Jenna?' Nicholas again said.

'That — that pot, Portelli,' Marc's anger mirrored the woman's as he pointed to the shattered pieces lying all around them, amidst piles of soil and greenery. 'It fell off, and only just missed Jenna. Where were you is what I'd like to know.'

'Marc,' Jenna spoke sharply, trying to warn him to be careful about what he said. In the short time that she'd known Nicholas, she'd learned to her cost, that he wasn't a man to be toyed with. And certainly not confronted in public with unsubstantiated allegations.

'I was inside.' Nicholas's eyes narrowed. 'Where should I have been?'

But Marc must have realised how impetuous he was being and didn't answer.

'Well?' Nicholas's voice rapped out.

'I-I don't know. I'm sorry.' Marc stammered. 'It's all been a shock.'

'Return to your duties then. And perhaps everyone else would also be good enough to return to whatever you were doing before this happened. You have my word, it will be fully investigated. You need have no worries either about your own or your children's safety.' Nicholas was in total control of the situation and, reassured, people began to gradually drift away. He swung back to Jenna, an ashen-faced Jenna by this time. 'What happened, exactly?'

Jenna told him. He stared up at the balcony above them, as if by doing that, he'd be able to see precisely what had happened. 'I've never known a pot to fall before. Was there anyone up there?'

'I don't know. I was watching the children in the pool. If Mr Blake hadn't shouted I wouldn't have known what was happening. It would have hit me.' Her shaking intensified. 'He was as puzzled as we are so I don't think he saw anyone. Nicholas, Marc didn't know what he was saying. It must have been the shock. He just needed to blame someone.

Nicholas turned his head and regarded her, a strangely still look to him. 'Blame someone? I assumed he thought I should have been around when the pot fell, as if I could have somehow prevented this?' He paused as enlightenment slowly dawned. 'He thinks it was me — that I pushed it over. Why would he think that?'

Oh no. Now she'd done it! Nicholas hadn't understood what Marc meant until she mentioned it. Why hadn't she kept her mouth shut?

She stuttered, 'Um, no. I-I don't know. Maybe I misunderstood.' She chewed at her bottom lip as she followed him into the bar and across to a secluded corner table.

He poured her a glass of brandy and

thrust it at her. 'Drink it. You're as white as a sheet.'

'I-I don't usually drink spirits,' she protested.

'You do now. It'll put some colour back into your cheeks.'

Jenna did as she was told. It seemed the easiest thing, and, truth to tell, after the first couple of mouthfuls, she did feel marginally better.

'Now, tell me again what happened — from the beginning.'

Once she'd finished, he said, 'I'll go and speak to the gardeners. They would have watered the plants up there this morning. Maybe they noticed something.' He stopped then as if something had just occurred to him. 'Do you, like Farruq obviously does, think that someone pushed it over? You can leave me out of the equation, I'd already left the dining room — right after you, in fact.' He spoke dryly.

She waited for him to say where he'd gone but when he didn't, she shook her head. 'I don't know what to think. It does seem an odd thing to have happened. The pot wouldn't simply topple on its own, surely? But why would someone do such a thing?'

The only person she could think of was Nicholas. And he'd said he was elsewhere. If only she could believe him. 'Has it ever happened before?'

'No, not in all the years that I've been here. And I agree it does seem strange. The gardeners never move them; they don't need to. And they're too heavy, in any case. They just water them — in situ. Could anyone have followed you out from England?'

'Why would they do that?'

He shrugged. 'Well, a disgruntled boyfriend might, I suppose; someone with a grudge, someone jealous of your good fortune? There must be someone that you've left behind that could be feeling aggrieved. Have you upset anyone?'

She was tempted to ask, 'What, someone other than you, you mean?' However, she contented herself with a slightly indignant, 'Enough to make them drop a pot on my head? I don't think so.'

He ignored that. 'So, no boyfriend?'

'Well, there was someone.' And, it was true, Rick had been upset, but he wouldn't sneak over here and do something like this. It would be totally out of character. Anyway, she didn't know that this morning's incident wasn't simply another accident. If indeed that's what the steps incident had been. Maybe now was the time to tell Nicholas about that? It would lend a semblance of credibility to her present alarm. 'But Rick wouldn't do anything like this.'

'Rick?'

'Yes, we went out together for a while. I ended it when I knew I was coming here.'

'And he took it well, did he?'

'We-ell, no. Look, let's just forget it, shall we?' She couldn't tell him about the fall down the cliff steps. She suspected he already thought she was over-reacting; being hysterical, even. Hearing her theory about that would have him believing she was paranoid as well. And if he detected her suspicion that he might be behind it, it would make their working relationship even more difficult than it already was, destroy it, even.

She had to believe that both incidents had been accidental. Otherwise how could she possibly remain here? 'There's no obvious explanation. As unlikely as it seems, the pot must have been off balance, somehow. I'll make sure I'm more careful where I stand in future.' If only it were that simple.

'Well, clearly Farruq doesn't believe it was accidental if you think he was blaming me.' There was an infinitesimal pause and then, 'Do you think it was me, Jenna?' And suddenly he was studying her intently, his gaze penetrating, as if he were trying to see inside her head.

'You're being ridiculous now. N-no.'

'You don't sound very sure. Do you

146

think I want rid of you, is that it? That I'd resort to murder to get my hands on 100% of the hotel?'

He sounded outraged. He had read her thoughts.

'What's Farruq been saying?' His eyes narrowed all of a sudden, making him look dangerous.

Jenna flinched. 'N-nothing. I don't know what you mean.'

'You don't, huh.'

'N-no.' Jenna suspected that he didn't believe her, that he guessed what Marc had told her. However, he must have decided to let it go for now because all he said was, 'I don't know whether anyone's mentioned it, but we hold a regular barbecue by the pool. It's on for tonight.'

'Yes, Bella said something about it.'

'Did she also mention it's your job to attend, supervise the running of it. Are you up to that?'

'Oh yes, definitely.'

'It'll take your mind off what's happened.'

True. As long as no-one tried to drown her in the pool, that was.

'I'll be in attendance, naturally. It starts at eight. You'll need to be there a good hour or two before to ensure everything's organised properly and ready. Your father used to enjoy doing that, every bit as much as he enjoyed the actual barbecue. He could be quite a charmer with the ladies — and they liked him. But maybe I shouldn't be telling you that?'

'No, that's fine. I want to find out as much about him as I can.'

'OK. Well, if you're sure you're all right now, I've got some jobs I must return to.' His look now was appraising rather than menacing. 'You've regained your colour, at any rate.'

'I'll be fine.' She'd drunk the brandy, much to her surprise, and it didn't seem to have gone to her head as she'd expected. It wasn't until she stood up that she realised she was wrong. She sat down again fast.

'Are you all right?' Nicholas asked.

'I'm not used to drinking brandy and it's made me a bit woozy.' She tried to stand again and once more experienced a disconcerting dizziness. 'I think I'd better sit here for a while,' she said.

'Come on, I'll take you up to your apartment. I would recommend a rest before the evening's festivities. I don't want to have to fish you out of the swimming pool. I'd probably get the blame for that too.'

His expression, and his words, were grim, and they echoed her own thoughts so exactly that she couldn't resist darting a glance at him. Was that the next plan of action? To drown her? Don't be stupid, she scolded herself. He'd hardly reveal his intention to his victim, would he?

Still, maybe it would be sensible to give the barbecue a miss? But then, if it was Nicholas behind things, he'd just find some other way to achieve his goal. Maybe she should concede defeat and sell out to him? Was it really worth risking life or limb for the sake of a share in a hotel? Surely her father wouldn't want her to?

But something, some inbuilt resistance to surrender in the face of intimidation and danger, insisted she was not going to be terrorised into running away. Her father had wanted her mother or her to inherit his share and that's what she was going to do.

She eyed Nicholas's set face. He wasn't a stupid man, and as she'd already told herself, he must know that if something untoward happened to her and he ended up with her share of the hotel, with his history of being thought responsible for his wife's sudden death, the finger of suspicion would point unwaveringly at him? And, let's face it, he'd always had a partner in the hotel, so why would he go to such extreme lengths to rid himself of her?

As she'd already concluded, the two incidents had to have been unrelated accidents. She'd simply been in the wrong place at the wrong time.

She got to her feet again, and once

more wobbled. Nicholas instantly put an arm around her waist, steadying her, holding her upright. Jenna, to her dismay, found herself nestling into his side. It was an instinctive reaction and one she hadn't been able to prevent. Despite the fact that she had suspected this man might be trying his best to kill her.

'Oh dear,' she gasped, 'I'm sorry about this.'

'Don't be,' Nicholas murmured, the words so low she could barely hear them. However, she couldn't miss the next ones. 'I'm rather enjoying it, as a matter of fact.'

Jenna didn't say anything, mainly because she didn't know what to say. His soft words had been the very last things she'd expected to hear after his earlier anger with her.

They reached her apartment door without further mishap. 'Give me your key,' he said.

Once they were inside, he helped her across to the settee that stood before the open French windows, arranging the cushions behind her head. 'Right. Have a nap and don't rush down to the pool. I'm sure they'll manage without you this once. They can always find me with any problems.' He paused, looking down on her, his expression a strange one. 'I'll have to remember not to give you brandy in future.'

She glanced up at him from beneath eyelids that were already drooping with fatigue. Drowsily, she murmured, 'See you,' before almost instantly falling into a deep, deep sleep.

Which was why she didn't see him, still standing, continuing to look down at her for several more minutes.

When she awoke an hour later, astonishingly all after-effects of the brandy had gone. It was the phone that woke her. Otherwise who knew how long she would have slept? She reached out a hand and lifted the receiver.

'Jenna?' a man's voice said.

'Yes.'

'It's me, Rick.'

She sat up smartly. 'Rick! What a surprise.'

'Pauline gave me your number. I hope you don't mind.'

'No, of course not.'

'I'm coming out.'

'Coming out? What on earth do you mean?'

'To Malta. To see you.'

An Unexpected Visitor

Jenna didn't know what to say. A visit from Rick? It had been the last thing she'd expected. As far as she was concerned, it was all over between them. She thought he'd understood that.

When her silence stretched on, he anxiously asked, 'Jenny? Is that OK?'

'Um — yes, yes, of course it is.' What else could she say? No, I don't want you to come? She couldn't do that, not to Rick. They might not be in love, but she hoped they could still be friends.

Jenna gave a great deal of thought to what she should wear for the barbecue that evening. Bella had told her that the women, especially, dressed up for the occasion. In the end, she plumped for a short, floral print, chiffon skirt and teamed it with a floaty top.

Nicholas was already there by the

time she arrived at the poolside; he'd clearly taken over her duties and was overseeing things. His first words were, 'I've asked the gardeners about the falling plant pot and no-one's admitting to having moved it or noticing anything amiss with it. Anyway, I've thoroughly checked the rest of them, they're perfectly balanced. There's no way any of them could topple over, so you can rest easy.'

His reassurances should have given Jenna peace of mind. But all she could think was that something or someone had made that pot topple.

'Anyway, are you OK now?'

'Yes, I'm fine. Now, what can I do to help?'

Within seconds, she was immersed in the various preparations that were entailed in organising a barbecue for a hundred or so people. The work drove everything else from her mind, falling boulders, falling pots, even Rick's imminent arrival. She didn't know what he was coming for, but she devoutly hoped it wasn't to try and persuade her to return to England and to him. Because he'd be wasting his time and money.

⋆　⋆　⋆

Apparently, a trio of musicians played throughout the evening, so Jenna concluded that there would be dancing. The gardens looked enchanting, due chiefly to the abundance of Chinese lanterns and fairy lights that were threaded through the trees and bushes that surrounded the pool, which also had underwater lighting. It leant the water an attractive golden shimmer.

Each table was laid with a pink cloth and napkins, and sported a large candle set in the centre of an arrangement of highly-scented flowers. It all made for a very romantic setting. She assumed it had been prepared while she'd slept.

Hotel guests had begun to drift in and settle themselves at the many tables that encircled the pool. The noise grew and intensified as the alcohol began to flow freely. Chicken, pork and several varieties of locally caught fish were cooking on the barbecue, producing mouth-watering aromas.

A thrill of excitement surged through Jenna. She was going to put her problems, her doubts and fears to one side for the evening and simply enjoy herself. She spotted Bernie and Bella, each with a man in tow, their husbands, presumably, heading for one of the two tables that had been especially reserved for the staff who were free to attend and their guests. Marc, of course, was working, waiting on the many tables, supplying drinks and canapés. Bella beckoned to Jenna.

'Over here, Jenna.'

She went over. Everything was organised and ready, so she could relax now. As she took a seat at the table, Nicholas joined them.

'Good, you've got yourself a seat. Give me another minute, I've got one last thing to do.'

Jenna was surprised. It sounded as if he intended to spend the evening with her. Which could only mean that he'd decided to forgive her her earlier suspicions of him over the plant pot. She watched him go. She'd have expected him to have some gorgeous woman in tow. Maybe that's who he'd gone to fetch.

But obviously not, because he was back and alone in record time, bearing two bottles of wine, the glasses were already on the table.

'OK,' he said, 'who wants red and who wants white?'

If Jenna was astonished at his easy familiarity, Bella and Bernie treated it as an everyday occurrence, and soon they were all laughing and joking together, with Nicholas revealing a previously unsuspected and ready wit. This was a side to him that Jenna hadn't yet seen; it was an immensely attractive and engaging side.

As was the manner in which he allowed his gaze to return to her, again and again, his expression a surprisingly warm one. Had he, at long last, decided to accept her presence here? Welcome it, even? She hoped so, she really did.

'Jenna,' he suddenly said, 'will you dance with me?' And before she could accept or refuse, he was on his feet and, with an outstretched hand, was pulling her up as well.

The effect was nothing short of electric.

Bella and Bernie both stopped talking mid-sentence as they watched the two people move on to the small dance floor that had been set up especially for this evening. Their glances at each other were full of excited speculation.

As for Jenna, she was suddenly sure that things were going to work out between her and Nicholas. She wouldn't listen to Marc any longer. Nicholas's wife's death had been a tragic accident, she'd lay money on that. The police would have charged him with murder otherwise.

The trio had struck up a slow tune and she had no hesitation in walking straight into Nicholas's open arms. Her heart was beating so fast, she almost expected it to leap from her breath.

She noticed Marc watching them, his gaze a brooding one. It struck her then that maybe he was jealous of Nicholas? After all, Nicholas had so much, while Marc, well, Marc had very little. He hadn't even had a father to speak of, and she knew what that felt like. It could also be the reason for Marc's continual bad mouthing of his employer, especially if he'd had hopes of something developing between himself and Jenna.

Maybe he'd anticipated Jenna and Nicholas getting things together eventually and had hoped to prevent it? Maybe he was hoping to secure a better life for himself, if he were romantically linked to a half-owner of the hotel?

Nicholas pulled her closer and began to steer her away from the watchful eyes of any staff that happened to be in their vicinity. Their steps were perfectly matched, their bodies seemed made to fit. In fact, anyone could have been forgiven for thinking they'd danced together many times before. Jenna certainly felt that way.

As he purposefully separated them from the other dancers, Nicholas laid his cheek against the side of her head. The smell of his aftershave filled her nostrils, and Jenna slid her arms up his chest and laced her fingers at the back of his neck. She detected the quickening of his breath at the same moment that hers did the same.

'Jenna,' she heard him murmur, 'are you happy here?'

'Yes,' she breathed, 'very.'

'You look lovely tonight.'

'Why, thank you, kind sir.' And she tilted her head back to laugh flirtatiously up at him, deliberately batting her eyelids in an exaggerated display of coquettishness.

He laughed, slightly shakily it had to be said. They'd moved quite a distance from the other guests and dancers by now, into the shadow of some trees. Her heart missed a beat. He'd done that quite deliberately, she had no doubt. He wanted to be alone with her, just as she wanted to be alone with him. But, against her will, a miniscule thread of worry resurrected itself — if he wished to hurt her, now was the time. No-one would hear her cries for help above the music.

But she swiftly discovered that it wasn't murder Nicholas had in mind, because his head lowered and his mouth hungrily covered hers. His hand cupped the back of her head, holding her firmly in position for his kiss.

A low cough sounded close by. Reluctantly they pulled apart. Marc was standing there, his face in shadow, but, nonetheless, obviously watching them, and obviously set on breaking up their moment. It seemed to confirm her suspicions of his jealousy over her.

'What do you want, Farruq?' Nicholas spoke angrily; harshly. His eyes were dark, treacly, their expression hooded.

Marc didn't answer straight away. Instead, he stepped forward so that his face was fully visible and shot a warning glance at Jenna.

'Well?' Nicholas demanded once more. 'And it had better be good.'

'Shall we begin serving the food — sir?'

Marc's tone was one of studied insolence. After his earlier implication that it had been Nicholas responsible for the falling pot, even if Nicholas himself hadn't comprehended that until Jenna heedlessly mentioned it, Jenna fully expected Nicholas to explode at this intrusion into their privacy. However, all he said was, 'For heaven's sake, if it's ready, yes.'

'Right, sir — madam.' He looked straight at Jenna now, his eyes glittering as he spoke with deliberate sarcasm. He'd never called her madam before. It must be his way of signalling his displeasure and jealousy.

He must have spotted her and

Nicholas dancing into the shadows and decided to halt whatever was happening. Or was she doing him an injustice and he had been genuinely fearful for her safety?

She groaned then. Oh Lord, and Rick was arriving in a couple of days. How was she going to deal with that? Three men, all intensely interested in what she was doing. And all vying to secure her affections? At any other time, she would have been flattered.

Marc turned away to return to his duties. Nicholas smiled ruefully at her. 'Time to return to the others?'

From then on, Marc hovered, coming up with excuse after excuse to come to their table. Did he sense what was happening to her? At one point, he hissed, 'What are you doing with him? Going off alone like that? He's tried to kill you twice already, have you forgotten that?'

In the end she retaliated, also in a low hiss, 'Marc, go and attend to the other guests. I'm fine. It wasn't Nicholas.'

Marc snorted contemptuously and left. He stayed well away after that.

But he needn't have worried. Because Jenna didn't dance again with Nicholas. He must have decided it was time he did his duty as hotel proprietor with several of the female guests that he'd got to know.

One in particular, Jenna could see, went out of her way to make the most of that. She pressed herself close to him, flirting madly. The fact that Nicholas appeared to be enjoying himself made Jenna's heart clench with anguish, especially when Bella murmured, 'He wants to watch himself with her. She was telling me she's recently divorced and is on the look out for a rich replacement.'

Jenna experienced an even sharper stab of pain at that. Still, she chided herself, it was her that he'd kissed, but she couldn't help wondering if he was merely a flirt, someone with an eye to the main chance. As she'd already reasoned, by hooking up with her, he'd stand a very good chance of gaining control of the entire hotel. Oh stop it, she wearily admonished herself. Give it a rest. You're as bad as Marc.

In the end, she was heartily relieved when the evening ended. Her head was aching, both from tiredness and the after-effects of drinking more wine than she was accustomed to. Before she left, she helped with the clearing away, and then, upset by the fact that Marc had completely ignored her throughout the tidying up, despite her frequent overtures to him, decided to have a short walk before retiring to bed.

* * *

There was no sign of Nicholas. Had the attractive divorcee enticed him away with her? She needed to think. A walk. That was it. It would cool her overheated emotions. The night was still extremely warm; so warm, that the air was almost sickly, scented as it was with the perfume of the many flowers that bloomed in such profusion all around her.

She strolled aimlessly. Where was Nicholas? She hadn't seen him for a while. Had he gone off with someone?

She stopped walking and looked around. Recollections of her other two 'accidents' swept into her mind and a surge of apprehension made itself felt. So much for her dismissal of them as just that — accidents. At the first indication of something unusual — threatening, her fears all flooded back.

'Who is it?'

No-one answered her. It must be an animal. There were bound to be many small creatures out and about at this time of night, all going about their business. She carried on walking and it was then that she caught a slight movement from the corner of her eye. A shadow danced beneath the branches of a tree and disappeared again.

Someone was there.

Another crack reinforced this conviction.

'Who's there?' Her tone reflected her alarm. It was shrill, fearful. 'I know there's someone there. Marc, is it you?' It would be just like Marc to follow her, guard her. But if it were Marc why didn't he answer her? He must know she'd be frightened.

Jenna shivered. An unexpected breeze had arisen, rustling the leaves on the trees. An owl called from a nearby branch. A bat suddenly streaked past her head, its pointed wings flicking her hair. 'Aah!' she shrieked, windmilling her arms wildly about her head. 'Get away from me.'

Thoroughly spooked by this time, she began to head back towards the hotel entrance. Again, something moved. She peered through the darkness, but couldn't see anything. Whoever, what-ever, it had been, had gone. Or maybe, there'd been nothing there in the first place?

With her emotions heightened by the events of the evening, it was possible that she'd imagined everything. The moonlight was bright and casting shadows everywhere, and the breeze was moving branches, maybe adding to them. It could be that what she'd believed was a person was nothing more than a trick of the light.

She broke into a jog. Trick of the light or not, she was taking no chances. She wanted to be inside and safe.

The hotel loomed before her. With the many lights that were always on beaming out, it looked like a haven of safety. She began to run, and within seconds, was through the main door and inside.

'Jenna! Whatever is it? You look terrified. Are you all right?'

It was Nicholas. He looked as out of breath as she was. Could it have been him? And he'd had to run too to make it inside before she did?

'Someone was out there — in the garden,' she blurted. 'Was it you, Nicholas? Was it?'

Rick Pleads His Case

Nicholas regarded her in astonishment. 'Of course it wasn't me. I'm here, aren't I?'

'Then why are you out of breath?' she demanded.

'I've been for a run. I do most nights.'

And Jenna belatedly realised he was dressed in track suit bottoms and a T-shirt. All black.

'It's the best time, I find. Cooler and quieter.'

'Oh yes,' she muttered, 'of course.' But he could also have dressed to merge into the shadows, to render himself virtually invisible.

'What happened, Jenna? I looked for you before I left the barbecue but couldn't find you.'

'Well, the last time I saw you, you looked so well — occupied,' she laced the word with sarcasm, disregarding the dangerous glint to his eye — he clearly knew to what she was referring, 'I decided I'd leave you to whatever it was you were doing. I helped with the clearing up in the kitchen and then went for a walk. But someone was there, watching me I thought. I called out but no-one answered. It was scary.' She hugged herself tightly, unable to control her violent shivering.

'And why would you think that was me?' The warmth within his eyes had been extinguished as he finally comprehended exactly what it was she was implying; they were almost transparent now, colourless, but despite that showing the definite beginnings of anger.

'I don't know. Coming in here and finding you, I suppose.'

'Don't you think I would have answered when you called if it had been me?'

'Yes, sorry — I don't know what I was thinking.'

'Maybe you weren't thinking,' he snapped.

'No, maybe I wasn't.'

'That's twice now I've been more or less accused of . . . Oh, go to bed, Jenna. Before we both say things we'll regret in the morning.'

The desire that had smouldered at her just seconds ago was gone, replaced by anger.

'Look,' he went on, more gently now in the face of her stricken look, 'it was probably one of the guests having a walk before bed.'

'But why wouldn't they have answered me when I called out?'

He shrugged. 'Who knows? Maybe they were meeting someone they shouldn't have been? I can't imagine anyone would deliberately try to frighten you. Why would they?'

'Why indeed?' she muttered to herself as she mounted the stairs to her apartment.

★　★　★

172

Bella took one look at her the next morning and said, 'Oh my! Bad night?'

'Yes. I seem to be having a few of those lately.'

'Look, why don't you take the day off? You haven't had any free time since you started helping out. It's well overdue and a break will do you good.'

The idea was tempting. Too tempting to resist. It would be good to escape the confines of the hotel. And maybe it would give her a fresh perspective on recent events? Ease her anxieties? But, apart from that, she'd seen virtually nothing of the rest of Malta. She'd read some guide books but that had been it.

'Do you know, I think I will. I'll go somewhere for the day.'

'Mdina is lovely. Or there's Valletta.'

She'd read about Mdina, The Silent City as it was known.

'There's an excursion to Mdina leaving from outside the hotel if you want to go along.' Bella checked her wristwatch, 'in half an hour.'

So that's what she did. She swiftly

changed back out of her work clothes into something cooler and more appropriate for sightseeing and climbed on to the tour bus along with everyone else. And just as she had hoped, the quiet peacefulness of the place was exactly what she needed.

Her anxieties were soothed by the tranquillity of the beautiful churches, the shady, narrow streets, and the occasional birdsong. A visit to the fortified ramparts of Bastion Square enthralled her with its panoramic views over the island and a cup of coffee on the terrace of the Fontanella restaurant revitalised her for more sightseeing.

As on the previous evening, once or twice she did feel she was being watched. She even thought she glimpsed a face at one point, peering at her round the corner of a building, but as it vanished before she had time to assimilate what she'd seen, or thought she'd seen, much less try to recognise it, she decided she'd been mistaken.

Nonetheless, she scanned the area all

around her but, seeing nothing untoward and absolutely no-one that she
recognised, she put it down to an
over-active imagination induced by the
fright and stress of the night before and
firmly dismissed it from her mind.

After all, she told herself, who would
go to the lengths of following her from
the hotel just to skulk around corners?
Certainly not Nicholas. If he even knew
where she was. And let's face it, he
must have far too much to do, keeping
their financial affairs in order. It was
their busiest time according to Bella.

* * *

By the time Jenna returned to the hotel
her spirits were restored, and she was
utterly convinced that the face she'd
glimpsed had nothing to do with her. It
had probably been a tourist who'd been
lost and had been trying to decide
which way to go next. Her fears of the
night before had been put well and
truly into perspective. She told herself,

over and over, that Nicholas simply wouldn't stalk her through the garden.

What she'd glimpsed, and it had been little more than a glimpse, just as it had been in Mdina, had been nothing more than the product of the night-time shadows, the breeze gently stirring the branches of the trees. Or, as she'd thought at the time, a small animal, moving along the ground, cracking twigs and rustling leaves as it went.

Nonetheless, when, upon her return, she spotted Rick standing in reception, she couldn't help but hurl herself at him, relieved at seeing someone she could trust, absolutely. 'You've arrived,' she cried. 'I wanted to be here to greet you. You're a day early.'

'Yes, I went to the airport and on to standby, just in case. And I've only just this minute arrived.' He grinned then. 'Mind you, if I'd known I'd receive such a welcome I'd have come long before this.' And he hugged her tightly. 'I was just asking this young woman where you were.' He was referring to

Bella, who was looking on, practically bug-eyed.

'Bella,' Jenna said, 'this is Rick, a very dear friend.' She resolutely ignored Rick's dismayed glance at her. He clearly still regarded himself as more than a friend. That had been a mistake, she belatedly admitted. But she'd been so thrilled to see someone from home, someone who couldn't possibly have been responsible for what had been happening, that she'd got carried away. Surely Rick would understand that and not expect more than she could give?

Bella smiled at her and handed her a key. 'Will you take him up?'

'Yes, of course.' She indicated the lift. 'This way, Rick.'

'By the way,' he said as he followed her, 'Pauline sends her love. She'll try to come out some time.'

'Great! I can't wait to see her. Rick,' she turned to him, 'you do realise I'll be working each day?'

'Yes, don't worry. I can amuse

myself. We can meet up each evening though, can't we?'

★　★　★

So that's how things worked out. Rick set off each morning, sightseeing in the car that he'd hired at the airport, and they ate together in the evening, always somewhere different.

They visited places that Jenna hadn't known existed, and certainly wouldn't have visited but for Rick.

He proved an entertaining companion, as well as being surprisingly knowledgeable about the island and its chequered history.

'I'm impressed, Rick,' she said at one point. 'I didn't think history was your thing.'

He merely grinned at her, relaxed and at ease in her company, his angry outrage at her leaving England evidently a thing of the past.

She hadn't seen anything of Nicholas. She didn't even know whether he

178

knew about Rick's arrival. She'd obviously angered him by thinking it could have been him in the garden.

She'd have to apologise, try to come up with some credible explanation for her suspicions. She couldn't tell him it had been Marc who'd fostered those suspicions because it would undoubtedly mean the sack for the younger man.

But towards the end of Rick's stay, things took a turn for the worse.

Just as she'd feared initially, her warm welcome and unmistakable pleasure in his company did revive Rick's hopes that things would work out between them and gradually his behaviour grew more romantic. Even so, for a time she managed to hold at bay any attempt to embrace her — until their last evening together, when his desire for her overwhelmed him and he pleaded with her to return to England.

They had taken their glasses of wine out to a secluded, vine-covered gazebo in the garden, well away from the hotel.

She later asked herself — whatever had possessed her? She couldn't believe she'd been so stupid, so unutterably thoughtless.

For once, they'd eaten in the hotel. Thankfully, Marc hadn't been on duty. She'd caught him, several times, staring at Rick in a strangely intense way, his dark eyes gleaming with what almost looked like hatred. It had made her extremely uncomfortable. Especially when Rick had asked, 'Why is that waiter glaring at me?'

'Oh, take no notice,' Jenna had told him. 'He's just watching over me.' She hoped that's all it was and he wasn't going to make trouble. She was beginning to suspect that Marc had a jealous nature, that a volatility that had, only recently, begun to show itself. Maybe, in her desire to have a friend in what had been to her initially an alien place, she'd heedlessly encouraged his hopes of a romance?

Rick had stared at her, and Jenna had wished she'd bitten her tongue out before uttering those careless words. Now, he'd want to know why someone should be watching over her.

Sure enough, 'Watching over you? What for? What's been happening?'

'Nothing. That was the wrong choice of words. He's just appointed himself my best friend, that's all. After all, I knew no-one and nothing about the island when I first arrived.'

'Hmmmph! Well, as long as that's all it is.' Eventually, she'd pacified him and Rick had ignored Marc's surveillance from then on.

But now, 'I still love you, Jenna,' Rick burst out. 'Please come back.'

'I can't, Rick. My life is here now. It's what my father wanted and, really, there's nothing in England for me.'

'What about me?' he indignantly demanded. 'I'm there. And don't say you don't feel anything for me, because . . . '

'Of course I feel something for you,' she interrupted, 'but not the sort of love you want me to feel. You're a dear friend and always will be. I thought you understood that. Please don't spoil things, we've had such a lovely time.'

'I know, but don't you see, that's because we're so well suited, so compatible,' he pleaded. 'Please, Jenna. Give us a chance. Come home.'

'No, I can't. I'm sorry.'

He reached out and grabbed her by the shoulders. 'Don't deny me, Jenna. I love you. I know I can make you love me — if you just let me.'

He pulled her close, knocking his glass over in the process. She heard the tinkle of it breaking and then saw the wine spill in a blood red pool on the wooden floor.

'Rick, please don't! Look, mind the broken glass!'

She began to struggle against his grip, but he seemed to have the strength of ten men and her attempts to free herself were having little or no effect.

He began to shower her with kisses, his hands imprisoning her, so tightly that she couldn't move.

'Rick!' she cried.

'What do you think you're doing?' The icy tones halted Rick.

Jenna looked up. Nicholas stood there, cold, accusing, contemptuous, staring down at her, with eyes as dark and as hard as granite as they absorbed the sight of the broken glass and the spilt wine.

She didn't have to wait long to find out.

'My word. You're quite a temptress, aren't you?'

His tone positively oozed disgust, reminding her of the way he'd sounded when he first found out who she was. He'd labelled her a gold-digger then, as well as a liar. She wondered what label he'd apply now?

Jenna felt the sting of tears. He thought she'd been encouraging Rick. And, in all honesty, that's the way it must have looked.

But Rick, in stark contrast to Jenna, was in no way intimidated. He got to his feet, yanking her up with him. He kept hold of her elbow — which was annoying, as all Jenna wanted was to hide behind him, away from Nicholas's ferocious glare. 'And who are you?' He was glowering, equally fiercely, at Nicholas. 'What do you mean — she's a temptress? And what the blazes is it to do with you anyway?'

'Absolutely nothing, if you discount the fact that I'm her partner in the hotel, that is, not romantically.' Nicholas's voice was perfectly even now; indifferent, in fact, although his gaze was still searing into her. The indifference actually hurt more than the contempt had.

'Nicholas, it wasn't how it looked.' Jenna said.

'Oh,' that maddeningly mobile eyebrow lifted, 'was it not? So, how was it then? Goodness, Jenna,' he evinced light surprise, 'you allow me to kiss you and then . . . ' He turned away from her. 'I presume you're Rick? I heard you were here.'

Rick turned to stare at Jenna now.

Jenna blushed scarlet. 'You were kissing him? When?'

'Last week, at the barbecue, before you came,' Nicholas smoothly told him. 'Obviously she's played us both for fools.'

Rick's face too now reddened — although not in humiliation as Jenna's had, his was the direct result of wounded outrage.

'My word, Jenna, it didn't take you long to replace me. How could you? And there I've been, missing you like crazy, wanting you back. While you . . .' Rick ran out of words with which to flail her. He let go of her hand, pushing her away from him.

Jenna staggered backwards, her face flaming even more hotly beneath the look that now adorned Rick's face. Nicholas thrust out a hand and steadied her. She pushed it away. She wanted nothing from him. Between the two of them, they'd made her feel like the worst sort of flirt.

In that second, she wanted nothing

more than to disappear off the face of the planet. So she did the only thing she could. She walked away with as much dignity as she could muster.

'Jenna,' she heard Nicholas sharply say. She ignored him and Rick's, 'Who else have you been messing with?'

She'd had enough for now, of both of them; her humiliation was complete. They had both accused and judged without allowing her any sort of defence at all.

In the aftermath of such complete arrogance, she wanted nothing more than to crawl beneath the bedcovers, where hopefully she would fall into a deep, dreamless sleep. Maybe if she could do that, things would look better in the morning?

But, to her dismay, sleep, as well as peace of mind, eluded her. Still burning at the recollection of both men's shocked expressions, and in particular, visualising, over and over, the contempt upon Nicholas's face as he stared at her, she tossed and turned endlessly.

Whatever he'd been starting to feel for her had been extinguished in one fell swoop, this time, sadly, through no fault of her own.

Nicholas despised her. As did Rick, apparently. A solitary tear made its way down her face. This wasn't how she'd wanted things to be. Maybe she should do what Rick wanted and return with him to England? But despite all that had happened earlier, and her feelings of shame and humiliation, that was the last thing that she wanted to do. And, in any case, Rick wouldn't want her with him now, not after this. No, more importantly than all of that, she'd feel she'd let her father, and herself, down.

* * *

In the end, she abandoned any attempt to sleep and instead decided to go through her father's things. She'd been putting it off and putting it off, reluctant to intrude upon his privacy. But, she admitted now, that she needed to know what had happened between her mother and him. What had driven him to leave them. And she desperately needed something, anything, to divert her thoughts from the disastrous events of the evening and the end of all her hopes for her and Nicholas.

She'd already been to see Max Pollacco, her father's solicitor, and the legal business concerning her father's will was being dealt with, including the completion of any documents that she needed to stay here. She wasn't sure what they were, but Max knew and was handling everything.

The first thing she did was to take out the two letters that she'd found when she first arrived. She started to open the earliest one, the one her mother had returned, the one that had been sent just months after Vince had left them.

She noticed now something that she hadn't previously upon finding it in the first place. It had been very carefully opened and then equally carefully resealed, so skilfully that, unless one looked closely, it was virtually undetectable. Which meant her mother must have read it. Jenna ripped it open and pulled the single sheet of paper out. The words revealed everything she'd wanted and needed to know.

Her father had written . . . *I was always afraid, right from the start, that the twenty year age gap between us would prove too great. Foolishly, I hoped it wouldn't matter. And I don't think it would have if you loved me the way I love you. But you don't . . . You want to party when all I want is an evening in — just the two of us. You knew full well how deeply your constant infidelity hurt me but still you carried on, flaunted it, in fact. I even doubted that Jenna was mine in the beginning, but she began to look so much like me that the doubts vanished.*

But I never stopped loving you. I still haven't. You don't care though, do you? The truth is you need far more than I ever can or ever could provide.

Which is why I decided the best thing I could do was disappear, quietly, and allow you your freedom. I didn't want any rows or unpleasantness over my decision, mainly because I didn't want Jenna upset.

As I said in my last letter, despite our differences, I hope you will allow me to see her. She could come and stay with me in Malta. I've bought a hotel, the Hotel Mursaloq, in the north west of the island. So there's plenty of people here to help me care for her. We could share custody.

Please don't ignore this like you did my last letter. At least reply. Let me know you're both OK, if nothing else. If you force me to, Helen, believe me, I'll apply to the court for a judge to decide who's the fittest person to bring Jenna up . . .

So it looked as if Nicholas might have been right. The moment her father mentioned having Jenna to stay and taking the matter of custody of her to the court, her mother had lived in fear of losing her daughter and so had started moving around.

It hadn't been any sort of fear of violence on the part of her husband. Jenna could at least feel gratitude for that.

If not for the fact that Helen had kept the fact that Vince was alive from her for so many years.

She opened the second letter, the one her mother hadn't received, judging by the unfamiliar handwriting on the envelope, that and the fact that this time it hadn't been resealed. She read . . . *please, Helen, please let me know you're both OK. Don't force me to go to the courts. That's the last thing I want — a bitter legal battle for custody. You're breaking my heart. I just want to see Jenna . . .*

There had been no other woman, that was very evident from the way her father had written. He had only wanted Helen. Something else her mother had lied about. Tears fell from Jenna's eyes at the clear evidence of her father's anguish. Helen had obviously moved by this time. If she'd read this heartfelt plea, surely she'd have relented and agreed to Jenna seeing her father?

With a deep sadness filling her heart, Jenna replaced the letters in the drawer in which she'd found them and there, she saw what she hadn't noticed before. Tucked away, right at the back, was a photograph album. She pulled it out and, with fingers that shook, opened it.

And there they were, all the missing pictures: her parents on their wedding day, on holiday together, laughing and happy. Then gradually, as she turned the pages, the happiness disappeared and misery took its place. There were photos of the three of them together, her father's face drawn and pale, her mother, blank-eyed, unsmiling, always looking in the opposite direction to Vince, her body language unmistakable. She'd rather be anywhere but with him.

The last few photos were just of Jenna. At what looked like about twelve months, eighteen months, two years

— running towards the camera, her chubby face beaming in delight, her dimpled hands outstretched. Finally, there were just blank pages.

Jenna wept again — for her father and his obvious unhappiness. And also for her mother, who'd clearly been every bit as unhappy. Yet, looking at this record of their all-too brief life together, she could understand why her father had left — although she wondered now if that had been the right thing to do. It hadn't eased his misery, that was only too obvious from his words and pleas. In fact, it had probably intensified it.

★   ★   ★

The following morning, she went to reception as usual. Rick would be leaving shortly and, sadly, all she felt was relief. He did come and bid her farewell, a cool farewell. She couldn't blame him. Not after what Nicholas had told him.

'I doubt we'll see each other again,'

he said. 'I wish you well.'

'Rick, it wasn't how Nicholas made it sound.'

'No? Well, it hardly matters. You made your feelings, or lack of feelings, about me very plain. Have a good life, Jenna, whoever you spend it with.'

'Rick, please. Don't go like this.'

But he did. He left swiftly and without as much as a wave or a backward glance. For the second time in a matter of hours, a great feeling of sadness engulfed Jenna. She'd meant what she'd said. He had been and still was a very dear friend. But that was all.

'He's Not My Type'

After that, Jenna immersed herself in fine tuning all she had learnt about the management of the hotel, trying to drive all thoughts of Nicholas from her mind. She wasn't very successful, chiefly because he was usually to be seen around somewhere and, of course, occasionally, they were forced to share the same office. That didn't happen often, due to Jenna being chiefly occupied at the reception desk or in other parts of the hotel, overseeing the smooth running of its daily affairs.

She also had trouble forgetting the unhappiness of her parents that the photographs and letters had so starkly revealed. How could her mother have been so harsh, so cruel? Maybe because, by the look of her in the photographs, she'd been every bit as unhappy as her husband? And, maybe, she'd blamed him for that?

There were always two sides to every story, and who was Jenna to judge, anyway? There was no doubt Helen had loved her daughter deeply. Otherwise why go to such lengths to keep her with her? Whatever her reasons had been — Jenna would never know now.

Nicholas remained cool and offhand whenever he and Jenna were forced to communicate. Marc remained changeable, one day moody and ill-tempered, the next smiling warmly at her. She didn't know what to make of him.

All in all, she began to feel abandoned and alone, and she yearned even more for the father she'd never had the chance to know. How different it all would have been if he'd still been alive when she was found. If she had him to turn to now — for advice, love.

Then, out of the blue, Pauline rang her. 'Jenna, it's me.'

'Pauline. Oh, it's so good to hear from you. How are you? How's work?'

'I'm fine, and work's — well, work,'

Pauline quipped. 'I miss you and the fun we used to have. The days seem very long without you here.'

'I know. Me too.'

'Oh, come on. I can't believe you find the days too long out there, with all that sun and sea. Life must seem like one long holiday.'

Jenna laughed. 'Well, not quite. I do have a job to do, you know.'

'I saw Rick the other day.'

Jenna felt her heart flip over, almost with a sense of dread. 'How is he?' Her question was nervously asked. She was still upset at the way they'd parted.

'Not too good. He says you're involved with this — this Nicholas Portelli.'

'That's not true. I'm not involved with anyone, well — other than in the course of running the hotel, obviously.'

'I don't think that's what Rick meant. He said Nicholas told him that you'd kissed.'

Jenna didn't know what to say. She couldn't lie to her best friend. The silence lasted for several seconds.

Pauline chuckled. 'So you did. You little devil, you.'

She'd phoned Pauline after she'd first arrived on Malta and told her that Nicholas wasn't the elderly man she'd expected, but instead was young and very personable. Pauline had yelled, 'Yes!' and Jenna had pictured her punching a triumphant fist into the air.

'What did I tell you?' she'd then said. 'Do you like him?'

'No, not at all. And he certainly doesn't like me. In fact, I suspect he's got me down as a complete idiot — and a deceitful one, too.' And she'd told Pauline what had happened. How, initially, she'd masqueraded under her mother's maiden name.

'Oh, Lord! Not a good start then?'

'You could say that.' And she hadn't spoken to her friend since. Which she did feel slightly guilty about. So, it was a huge relief to hear from Pauline now. She'd sent a postcard or two but that had been all.

'So . . . ' she could hear the grin in her friend's voice now, 'things have improved between you since your first faux pas — if you've been kissing. No wonder Rick was upset.'

'Pauline,' she spoke sharply in her own defence, 'Rick's upset because I wouldn't have him back and then he tried to force himself on me. Nicholas saw us and was furious, which was when he told Rick we'd kissed.'

Pauline was shocked, so much so, that she clearly missed Jenna's final low-voiced admission. 'He's not that sort of guy — is he?'

'I didn't think so.' She sighed, wondering whether to confide her growing feelings for Nicholas to Pauline.

'And now?'

She decided not to. 'Nothing. Nicholas has reverted to the wrong side of glacial in his dealings with me.'

'And that bothers you?'

'Only in that we have to work together, so it does make life rather awkward.'

'So — no feelings for him, then? You know, the loving kind?'

'Good Lord, no! He's not my type.' She heard herself lie and closed her eyes in shame. She'd never, ever lied to Pauline before. They'd shared everything, every little secret, no matter how dire. What was happening to her? To her sense of what was right or wrong?

'We're just business partners, that's all.' Maybe she should tell Pauline of her fears regarding Nicholas? About the 'accidents' that had happened? Or maybe not? She had no proof that they'd been anything other than that.

'Anyway,' Pauline went on, 'changing the subject completely, I thought I'd spend my week's holiday with you.'

'Oh, Pauline,' Jenna cried, 'that would be wonderful. When?'

'Um — next week? Is there a room available?'

'You can stay with me in my apartment. As long as you don't mind a futon in my room?'

'That sounds perfect.'

★　★　★

Jenna felt as excited as a young girl over the prospect of her friend's arrival. On the day Pauline was due to arrive, she made up the futon and filled the apartment with flowers out of the hotel's gardens. Their scent, rich and heady, perfumed the rooms, even though all the French windows were standing open to the hot summer breeze.

Pauline was taking a taxi from the airport, and, if all went to plan and there was no delay on the flight, she should reach the hotel by mid-afternoon. Jenna carried on with her work, desperately trying to quell her excitement at the idea of having her dearest friend with her.

To be able to look at her familiar face, to know she had an ally here with her — it was an overwhelming feeling. So, it wasn't surprising that Jenna's glance was drawn, again and again, to the hotel doors.

Then, suddenly, there she was. The heavy doors sprang open and Pauline strode through, her face wreathed in the saucy grin that Jenna was so familiar with, dragging a huge case behind her across the tiled floor. Columbus, the parrot, emitted such a loud squawk, that even if Jenna hadn't been glancing at the doorway for the umpteenth time, she would have known that someone had arrived.

Pauline let go of the case and spread her arms wide. 'Here I am, at long last. Whew! It's hot enough to fry egg and bacon on that pavement outside.'

Jenna ran across to her and hugged her tightly.

'Hey! Whoa. Do you want me to stop breathing?'

'Sorry.' Jenna released her friend. 'But it's so good to see you.'

And it really was. This time she really did have someone she could trust with her, albeit only for a short while. She felt secure, safe — it was wonderful. Jenna felt her eyes stinging with tears.

'Hey, hey! What's this?' Pauline regarded her. 'Missed me that much, huh?'

'Oh, yes, yes!'

'Are you OK?' Pauline looked anxiously at her, obviously sensing her extreme emotion.

'Yes, I'm fine. Ignore me — it's the excitement of having you here.'

'Right.' Pauline looked around then for the first time. Her eyes widened. 'It's like a jungle in here. There's even a parrot!'

'I know. I couldn't believe it either the first time I saw him.'

'Met Tarzan yet? Because if you have, I definitely want an introduction.'

'You haven't improved, have you?' Jenna laughed. 'Come on, I'll take you up to the apartment. Bella,' Jenna called, 'can you manage for a while?'

'Of course,' Bella replied with an answering smile, 'take as long as you want. You're the boss, after all.'

* * *

Once they'd got Pauline unpacked and settled, they sat on the balcony outside the apartment, each with a glass of white wine.

'You've really landed on your feet here, gal,' Pauline exclaimed.

'It's wonderful, isn't it? And half of it's mine.'

They laughed again, Pauline slightly enviously, Jenna with unadulterated delight.

'My cup runneth over,' she quoted. 'Sun, sea, my own business and my dearest friend here with me.'

'So,' Pauline eyed her speculatively, 'fill me in on this Nicholas Portelli. Don't leave anything out.'

'There's not much to tell, really. We work together — that's it.'

'Right — yeah,' Pauline scoffed. 'So if that's all it is, how come you kissed, eh?'

'It was a brief flirtation, nothing more. One evening at the barbecue.' Jenna couldn't meet her friend's eye as she inwardly groaned. Yet more lies. She and Pauline had never had secrets. What had changed? Other than the fact that she was here on Malta.

'Oh-ho. That raises an interesting question. Would he be mine then?'

'You'll have to make up your own mind about that.'

Pauline eyed her over the rim of the wine glass. 'So — I wouldn't be treading on your toes then?'

Jenna shrugged and took an extra large swig of her wine — only to swallow it the wrong way and start to choke.

Pauline slapped her hard on the back. 'The idea that upsetting, huh?'

'No, no,' Jenna energetically protested as soon as she had the breath to speak once more, 'not at all. He's all yours. You'll meet him tonight. It's barbecue night.'

* * *

That evening, she and Pauline both donned their finery, Pauline having brought along almost every garment she currently possessed. Which, of course, necessitated trying each one on, in her enthusiastic and long-winded quest for the perfect look.

'You look gorgeous,' Jenna eventually told her. And she truly did. Nicholas would have to be only half a man not to be attracted to her. Jenna felt her spirit sink.

'So do you,' Pauline generously told her.

'Do you think so?' Jenna glanced down over herself.

'I do. I often thought you were a bit too slender. You've filled out very nicely.'

Jenna walked across to the full length mirror and tried to view herself through Pauline's eyes. She did look better.

'So, are we ready then?' Pauline asked. 'I can't wait to meet Nicholas.'

She didn't have to wait. By the time they got down to the pool side, he was there, striding around in that confident, self-assured manner of his.

'Oh wow, smell that,' Pauline groaned. 'I could easily eat the whole lot. Oh boy! Is that Nicholas?' Pauline was staring over at Nicholas, her face a picture of delight. 'Are all Maltese men this gorgeous?'

'Yes, that's Nicholas,' Jenna resignedly told her. She should have known Pauline would go for him, big time. Now, she'd have to watch her closest friend making a play for the man that Jenna was beginning to want herself.

'How on earth do you get any work done with him there?'

'He is good looking, I suppose.'

'You suppose!' Pauline chuckled. 'Who are you kidding? You'd have to be made of stone not to be affected by him.'

'After a while you don't really notice his looks,' Jenna said, desperately trying to sound as if she meant it.

Pauline gave her a droll look. 'Yeah! Right. Look, kiddo, you can fool yourself, but you can't fool me. We've been friends too long.'

'I'm not trying to fool anyone,' Jenna sharply said.

She was saved from having to utter any more untruths by the sight of Nicholas glancing their way, looking away, and then turning instantly for a second longer look. Despite this, he didn't appear to miss as much as a breath. Annoyingly, Jenna decided.

Did he always have to appear so composed? She'd just once like to see that self-possession shaken, that confidence dented. Was that too much to ask? Apparently it was, because he issued one more order to the chef before striding across to the two women.

A Tangled Web

'I assume this is your friend,' Nicholas smoothly said, an appreciative grin widening his mouth as he turned his gaze on to Pauline. Pauline had cast her completely into the shade. 'Hi, I'm Nicholas Portelli. It's a pleasure to meet you; a real pleasure.'

'Pauline.' Pauline introduced herself with a pouting smile.

Not surprisingly, Nicholas's glittering gaze lingered on her as a lazy smile curved his lips. Jenna might as well not be there. She tightened her mouth angrily. How had he known Pauline was even coming, let alone that she'd arrived? Bella? It must have been. Certainly Jenna hadn't told him, she had barely seen him to tell him. And look at him now, bowing his head over Pauline's hand, brushing the back of it with his mouth. So predictable. She glared at the top of his head.

A mistake.

Because, completely unexpectedly, he straightened and glanced sideways at Jenna, literally catching her in the act. It brought a disconcerting little smile to his lips, despite the fact that Jenna had instantly rearranged her features into an expression of total indifference. He'd seen straight through her pretence, as she might have known he would. His glance flicked over her, but as he almost at once looked away again, she could only assume he was unimpressed. And who could blame him, with Pauline standing alongside her? Jenna had been cast aside, forgotten.

'Jenna, I hope you've given Pauline one of our better rooms.'

'She's staying with me,' Jenna snapped.

'Oh, good.'

Somehow, his words didn't ring true.

'Take Pauline to that table over there.' He indicated a table set beneath a tree and a little apart from all the other tables. 'I'll join you in a second or two, It'll just be the three of us.' He then bestowed a warm smile upon Pauline. 'I want to hear all about you and your friendship with Jenna.'

Over my dead body, Jenna mutinously vowed. As he walked away from them, Jenna muttered, 'You tell him nothing, you hear. It's none of his business what I did before I got here.'

'Don't worry, my lips are sealed — but about what?' Pauline looked puzzled. 'You don't have any deep, dark secrets. Or at least if you do, you haven't shared them with me.'

'He's just fishing. I might have exaggerated my previous experience in the world of hotel management.'

Pauline threw back her head and laughed loudly. 'Is that all? Anyway, you don't need to worry. I don't intend to waste any time talking about you. Do you know, I think he likes me. What do you think?'

Jenna didn't reply. A stab of something that closely resembled jealousy pierced her chest, effectively silencing her as she led Pauline to the table that Nicholas had indicated.

She'd been sorely tempted to ignore his order and find another table, as far away from him as humanly possible, without having to go to the lengths of sitting on the pavement outside the hotel. However, she thought that Pauline might have something to say about that, so she did as she'd been told.

The table was beautifully laid with a starched white cloth and napkins, silver cutlery and crystal glasses — as well as a truly massive arrangement of flowers. All in Pauline's honour? It certainly wouldn't be for her, Jenna. She'd been consigned, more or less permanently it would seem, to the dog house.

She glowered at the candles already lit and emitting a softly flickering glow as well as a seductive perfume. He'd certainly pulled out all the stops. There were also two bottles of wine, already uncorked. 'Wow!' was Pauline's soft exclamation. 'Romantic, huh?'

By the time the two women had seated themselves, Nicholas arrived back. 'Pauline.' Again, he gave that slow, tantalising smile, as he pulled his chair as close to Pauline's as he could physically get, and proceeded to slide his arm along the back of her chair. Jenna gritted her teeth. For two pins, she'd leave the table and retire to bed.

'Red or white?'

'Red, please.' Pauline stopped just short of actually batting her eyelids at him. Again, Jenna gritted her teeth.

'Jenna?' His gaze cooled as it rested upon her. She thought she detected contempt flickering within it — just momentarily. It confirmed her suspicion that all the trouble had been taken for Pauline, not for her.

He clearly still hadn't forgiven her for what he obviously viewed as her outrageous behaviour with Rick, that and her suspicion, foolishly put into words, that it could have been him stalking her in the garden.

'Red, too, please.' She kept her tone

even. Not for anything would she allow him to perceive her unhappiness at his flirtation with Pauline.

He filled her glass, and then looked straight at her. Something in his expression told her he knew exactly what she was feeling. A glint of what looked suspiciously like satisfaction lit his eyes, and then, almost instantly, was gone again, leaving Jenna to wonder if she'd imagined it? Or was he deliberately toying with her emotions? Leading her on, then cruelly slapping her down again? Punishing her, in other words?

$\star$ $\star$ $\star$

From that moment on, the evening went downhill for Jenna. The second that the group began to play, Nicholas and Pauline were on their feet dancing.

Jenna couldn't, in all honesty, blame her friend. She'd told her she wasn't interested in Nicholas, not in a romantic way. And if Nicholas was indeed trying to punish her, what better way than to hurl his attraction to her best friend in her face?

'Jenna, will you dance with me?'

Jenna looked up, straight into Marc's eyes, eyes that reflected his sympathetic understanding of the pain she was enduring. Which was surprising, taking into account his increasing volatility. Just yesterday, he'd ignored her, the day before that, he'd been charm itself. She decided to accept him as he was for the moment, accept that he was still a teenage boy, with all the moodiness that that could entail.

'You look lonely.' His glance strayed to where Nicholas and Pauline were dancing. 'Please, come and dance,' and he held out his hand, his expression one of muted appeal.

Jenna stood up. 'Thank you, Marc, I'd like that,' and her glance too strayed to her friend and Nicholas. Only to wish, a second later, that she hadn't bothered. For they were dancing so closely that one would have been hard put to it to slide as much as a sheet of paper between them.

Pauline was laughing up at something that Nicholas had said and Nicholas was looking down at her, and smiling back.

It reminded her of her and Nicholas's very first meeting. He didn't smile at her like that any more. She hardened her heart and allowed Marc to take her in his arms and guide her to the area reserved for dancing.

She felt Nicholas's gaze upon her, sensed his disapproval. She ignored it, she and Marc were both off duty. They could do as they pleased, and there was nothing Nicholas could do about it.

Marc proved an extremely adept dancer, with a strong sense of rhythm. Jenna soon found herself laughing and flirting, and actually enjoying herself. So much so, that she didn't notice Pauline and Nicholas calling a halt to their dancing and moving back to the table. It took Pauline calling, 'Go, Jenna, go,' to make her look over, only to find herself the object of

Nicholas's dark glare.

Determined not to be inhibited by his disapproval, she threw herself even more energetically into the dance. Marc laughed down at her and murmured, 'Oh dear, I don't think the big boss approves.'

'He may be your big boss, he's certainly not mine.'

Marc laughed and pulled her close, dropping a kiss upon her cheek. Jenna knew she shouldn't but she snuggled closer. Marc's hold was tightening round her when a voice as cold as the Arctic interrupted them.

'Excuse me, Jenna, I'd like a word,' and he grabbed hold of her arm, yanking her away from Marc.

'How — how dare you?' Jenna gasped, as she fought to keep her balance.

Nicholas regarded her coldly, not reacting in any way to her cry. Instead, he pulled her into his own arms and began to dance her away from the younger man. 'I dare because your behaviour is hardly seemly.' His tone was as icy as his look had been.

'What behaviour? We were just dancing, enjoying ourselves — Marc?' She swung to appeal for his support, but Marc had gone. It was as if he'd never been there. She turned back to Nicholas. His eyes gleamed darkly, his top lip was curled. 'He's gone. Satisfied?' she furiously demanded. 'What is your problem with Marc?'

'My problem,' sarcastically mimicking her, 'is the sight of my business partner cavorting with a younger member of her staff.'

'Cavorting! And anyway,' she decided to put her thoughts into words. See how he liked that. 'I was only doing what you and Pauline were doing.'

'Ah, but Pauline doesn't work for me. That's the difference, and if you can't see that, then . . . '

'Then what?' she blurted.

'Then maybe you shouldn't be in a managerial position. You were blatantly flirting with him. What do you think that looks like to the rest of the staff? I've already warned you once.'

'How dare you?'

He sighed wearily. 'You've already asked me that once.'

'Who do you think you are? I can have any position I want. I do own practically half of this hotel. Or had you forgotten that?'

Astonishingly, they had carried on dancing throughout this bitter exchange, but Jenna stumbled now, so furious was she. Nicholas's arm instantly tightened about her, supporting her, and then pulling her in so that their chests slammed together. Jenna's breath caught in her throat at the look that was in his eyes as they made contact. It blazed at her, but with what? Hatred? Passion?

'No, I hadn't forgotten.' His eyes darkened, his voice became low and throaty. 'I tell you these things because I'm . . .'

'Hey, you two! What's going on?'

It was Pauline. A Pauline who was

distinctly miffed, judging by the tone of her voice.

'Nothing is going on,' Nicholas answered, still staring down at Jenna, his expression a bleak one all of a sudden, empty of any emotion — anger or otherwise.

Jenna wondered what he'd been about to say when Pauline had interrupted. Not that she cared. If he was going to go on being so — so dictatorial, then she could do without it. She wrenched herself free of his grasp and said, 'Do you know, I'm tired. I think I'll leave you to it.'

'Jenna!' Pauline said, surprised. 'It's only ten o'clock. The party's just starting.'

'Not for me. It's over for me.' And she glowered at Nicholas. This was all his fault. 'You stay, Pauline. I'm sure Nicholas would be heartbroken if you left too. I'll see you later.' Without another word, she stalked away.

'You're In Love
With Him'

'Jenna?' Pauline again cried. But, for the first time ever, Jenna ignored her. Tears were stinging her eyes, tears that she wanted no-one else to see, not even her closest friend. Which was stupid. And what was she crying about, anyway?

She dashed away the moisture that insisted on settling on her cheeks. What made the whole thing even worse was that, deep down, she knew he had a point. It had been unseemly behaviour on her part, and it hadn't been fair to Marc. With her heedless behaviour, she'd encouraged whatever hopes he'd been entertaining about her and himself. It hadn't just been thoughtless; it was worse than that, it was downright cruel.

He was just a boy. She should be

ashamed of herself — and she was. It wasn't like her to behave in such a manner. She'd done it simply to annoy Nicholas and that made the whole thing even more reprehensible. Well, she'd certainly succeeded in her intention. Nicholas was annoyed all right. What had gone wrong? she wearily asked herself. She'd come to Malta with such high hopes and they were all gradually turning to dust. Mainly due to her own actions, she admitted miserably.

She buried her face in her hands as the lift carried her up to the top floor and her apartment. Pauline would probably be hot on her heels, demanding to know what had sent her scurrying off like a frightened cat. She needed time to calm herself, dry her tears. She fled into the bathroom and locked the door behind her.

A cold shower restored some of her composure, then she dressed herself in a pair of shorts — it was still very hot despite the late hour, and a top. Only then did she feel ready to face her friend.

She went into the sitting room. It was empty. So Pauline had declined to follow her. Jenna knew she'd told her to stay, but — Nicholas. Of course. Pauline wanted to be with Nicholas. As much as Nicholas had seemed to want to be with Pauline. Jenna felt the hurt begin; the disappointment. She hadn't seen Pauline in weeks. She'd have thought her friend would have wanted to spend their first evening with her.

She walked out on to the balcony. The full moon was painting a silver pathway across the inky water, the dazzling centrepiece to a galaxy of stars. She could see the lights of what she guessed were a couple of fishing boats way out, but other than that the sea was dark and empty.

Usually she loved this scene, but tonight she would have given anything to have been overlooking the pool side. To see what Nicholas and Pauline were doing. She'd have to go down to do that, and that was the last thing she wanted to do. She could just see the self-satisfied expression that would light Nicholas's face.

Instead, she poured herself an extremely large glass of wine, all the time, struggling with her feelings of hurt anguish at the thoughts of Pauline and Nicholas together. A small sob made its way up her throat. This situation was of her own making entirely. She'd told Pauline to go ahead.

She sat on the balcony, unhappy and alone, waiting for her friend to return. When she didn't arrive, Jenna threw herself on to her bed, still dressed, and fell into a heavy, dream-filled sleep.

She dreamt her father was still alive and was here with her, holding her close, telling her not to worry, he loved her, even if Nicholas didn't. The tears slid from beneath her eyelids even in her sleep.

* * *

The next morning, Jenna woke to find Pauline already up and dressed. She hadn't heard her come in the night before. 'Pauline, have you been with Nicholas?'

'Of course I haven't. I've only just met the man, for heaven's sake. What do you think I am? Anyway, he left right after you did.'

'What? He left?' A surge of something that felt very much like elation flooded through Jenna.

'Yeah. He looked more miserable than you do now.'

'But why?'

'Because you'd gone, I should think. The man's crazy about you, for goodness sake.'

'Are you mad?'

'I don't think so. I think he was jealous of you and that young chap — what's his name?'

'Marc.' Jenna spoke slowly, she couldn't believe what Pauline was telling her.

'I mean, the way he looked when you

went was enough to show me how he felt. And you feel the same way, don't you?'

'No-no, I don't,' Jenna protested — in vain.

'Oh, come off it, Jenna. You're in love with him. Madly, deeply, everlastingly, I shouldn't wonder. It's written all over you.'

Jenna again groaned. Was she that obvious? Pauline was right, of course. About her feelings, at least. She wasn't so sure she'd read Nicholas's correctly. He'd just looked angry to Jenna, not at all like a man in love. And how on earth could she have fallen in love with a man that she wasn't sure wasn't trying to harm her? Maybe she should confide in Pauline, share her doubts, her suspicions.

No, she couldn't. What if Pauline then accused Nicholas? And Jenna wouldn't put it past her. If it had been Pauline who it had been happening to, she'd have long ago confronted Nicholas with her suspicions.

'Tell him how you feel.'

'I can't.'

'Believe me, he feels the same. I'd put money on it.'

'Huh!' Jenna snorted. 'I wouldn't. Honestly, you haven't heard the way he talks to me. His behaviour is not the behaviour of a man in love — whatever you think.'

'Well . . . ' For the first time Pauline looked doubtful.

'See, you aren't sure, are you?'

'So it wasn't jealousy of Marc then that provoked all that rage?'

'No. He's big on keeping your distance from your employees. Especially ones who are younger than yourself. Anyway, to change the subject, who did you spend the rest of the evening with?'

'I met this dishy chap. He's single, and gorgeous, and . . . ' Pauline paused at this point, looking at her friend somewhat uncertainly, 'I said I'd go out for the day with him, if you don't mind, that is.'

'No, of course I don't mind. You're here on holiday. And I've got work to do.'

And that was that. Pauline spent the remainder of her holiday, apart from a couple of evenings which she spent with Jenna, falling in love. She did return each night to the apartment, but it was usually long after Jenna had fallen asleep. And as for Jenna, she spent the week trying to keep out of Nicholas's way. She more or less succeeded as far as Nicholas was concerned.

Marc seemed to show up everywhere she went. Sunny, smiling, his moodiness apparently banished for now. This must be down to her behaviour on the evening of the barbecue. Just as she'd feared, it had renewed his hope of some sort of relationship developing between them, something more than mere friendship. His hopes were sufficiently high to inspire him to ask her to his home — for tea, no less.

'I've told my mother so much about

you that she wants to meet you,' he said.

'I don't think so, Marc,' she gently said. She had to stamp on those hopes — and hard, as cruel as that seemed to her. Which meant that she wanted to do it without hurting his feelings too deeply.

'Please,' he begged. 'She worked for a brief time for your father, as you know, and she would very much like to meet his daughter. That is all. Nothing more. She had great respect for your father. I have taken the liberty of saying you will come. She is very excited about it.'

In the end, and because she really didn't want to hurt him any more than she already had, she agreed to go. She also didn't want to disappoint his mother.

'Splendid,' he beamed. 'We will go this afternoon. Mama is expecting us. I finish work at three — and your friend has gone home, so there is nothing and no-one to keep you here.'

'Oh, I'm not sure about today,' Jenna

weakly protested. 'I have to work.' Really, what was the rush? It was all happening too fast for her liking. She was beginning to feel stampeded.

'Come, come,' Marc chided her, 'you are the boss. You can do what you want.'

She couldn't legitimately dispute that. So, 'Oh, very well. I'll meet you in reception at three-fifteen.'

It was just her luck, of course, that at that second precisely, Nicholas should be standing in the area talking to one of the guests. When he noticed her and Marc together and walked towards the main doors, moreover, his brow lowered and his eyes turned steely.

'Jenna, just a moment.' And he made his excuses to his companion and strode across to her. 'Has Pauline gone? I haven't seen her around.'

'Yes, she went a couple of days ago.' So he'd been looking out for Pauline, had he? He wouldn't know she'd left because she wasn't a paying guest and so hadn't formally checked out. But why hadn't he simply asked Bella? She knew. Anyway, whatever his interest in Pauline's whereabouts seemed to make a nonsense of the theory that he cared for Jenna.

'I hope she enjoyed her stay sufficiently to return sometime.'

'I'm sure she did.' His words had just confirmed her own conviction that Pauline was way off course. It had been Pauline he'd been interested in, despite his leaving the barbecue early too. He probably hadn't wanted to be too obvious about things. She felt the misery settle upon her.

'Good; good.' His gaze strayed to Marc and narrowed ominously. 'And where are you going now? So early in the afternoon?'

Surely he wasn't going to demand that she finish the working day? 'Well, it is after three.'

'I know that. My mother did teach me to tell the time.'

Jenna mutely simmered at his sarcasm. 'Marc's mother has expressed a wish to meet me. She knew my father, but then I expect you know that too.' Her sarcasm wasn't lost on him. His darkened gaze captured hers and held it.

It was Jenna who turned away towards Marc. 'Are you ready, Marc?'

Marc's expression surprised her. It was one of unadulterated triumphalism. Gloating, even. Again, Jenna questioned the wisdom of what she was about to do. Had he invited her out simply to get one over on Nicholas? Or had his mother really asked to meet her? She was no longer sure.

An Uncomfortable Meeting

It didn't take them long to reach Marc's home, a small, white walled house, standing back from the road, with a pretty, well tended garden. The bougainvillaea that seemed to be everywhere on the island had intertwined with cream roses and scrambled in lavish profusion around the bright green door, to then clamber almost all of the way up the front wall of the house.

The door was already open and, as Jenna studied the building, a woman appeared. A woman who stood in silence and, in return, made a careful study of Jenna. Her stare took in every inch, from the top of her head to her feet, making Jenna glad that she'd opted for a smart linen trouser suit, rather than the jeans and T-shirt she'd originally pulled from the wardrobe. She had no idea why she'd done that. A sixth sense, maybe, that had warned her that this woman would expect her to have made an effort.

The woman herself was attired in a neat blouse and skirt, with hair that was immaculately arranged in a knot on the nape of her neck. She didn't seem to have given anything of her looks to her son. She was blonde where he was dark and her eyes were a strangely pale blue, almost transparent, as opposed to Marc's deeper blue. Jenna felt that if she got up close, she'd be able to see her own reflection in them.

Jenna smiled and held out a hand. 'Hello, I'm Jenna.'

'Yes, I know who you are.' Her voice was low, throaty, and, surprisingly, her English was as impeccable as her son's. She took Jenna's hand in a limp clasp before instantly letting it go again. 'I'm Marina, Marc's mother. Please come in.' And she stood to one side to allow the young couple in.

The house's interior was unusually dark, considering the brilliance of the day, but that was due, Jenna saw, to the blinds on the windows being almost completely pulled down. There was a gap at the bottom of maybe six inches. It let in just enough light to see by.

'I don't care for the sun,' Marina said, obviously in response to Jenna's glance at the shaded windows. 'It fades everything and I can't afford to keep replacing things. Please — sit.'

It was an order, not an invitation, so Jenna took the seat indicated. She smiled, hoping to warm the noticeable chill of the atmosphere, a chill that wasn't entirely due to the darkness of the room. That gloom seemed exacerbated by the open hostility that was emanating from the woman. So powerful, Jenna could almost touch it.

'You are older than I expected,' Marina bluntly said, after a further study of her features.

'Oh, really.' Jenna glanced uncertainly at Marc, but there was no help to be had there. He was staring at the floor and said nothing. 'Didn't Marc tell you?'

'Marc tells me nothing,' the older woman said, her tone laced with disapproval. 'He just said that he has someone he wants me to meet.'

'Oh.' Jenna felt a deep dismay. Marc had said it was his mother who wanted to meet her. He'd lied. Again, she glanced at Marc. Still he refused to meet her look. Why had he lied? Because he'd known she wouldn't agree to come if he'd said it was all his idea? But that wasn't the only thing he'd lied about. He'd also said that his mother was excited at the prospect of meeting Jenna.

Anyone less excitable than Marina, Jenna had yet to encounter. There was an almost unnatural calm about her, a coolness, even when criticising her son. Jenna felt a pang of misgiving. 'Marc?'

He did look up then, but not at

Jenna, at his mother. His expression was one of deep displeasure. 'Mama, that is not quite true, is it? You wished to meet Jenna now, didn't you?' Marc's olive skin had taken on a tinge of scarlet. Was it anger that had provoked that or embarrassment?

Marina sniffed loudly and turned her head away, her only response to her son's accusation a brief shrug of her shoulders. She clearly didn't deem it worthy of a verbal response.

Jenna took the opportunity to make a closer inspection of the woman. She looked to be well into her fifties, considerably older than Jenna had expected. Old, anyway, to have a nineteen-year-old son. Her skin was good, she obviously looked after herself.

The things that betrayed her age were the deep lines around the eyes and mouth, and the tell-tale signs of sagging about the jawline. But for all that, she was an attractive woman. She must have been quite stunning when younger. Jenna wondered why she'd never married? Why Marc's father had so callously deserted her?

'Well,' Marina got to her feet, 'I will get the tea. Marc, come and help me, please.' Again, it wasn't a request, it was an order.

Jenna stumbled to her feet. All of a sudden, she couldn't wait to get out of this house. She'd never felt more unwelcome anywhere in the whole of her life. She shouldn't have come, she should have trusted the instincts which had warned her not to. 'Look, there's really no need to go to any trouble. I have to get back anyway.'

Marina turned her head and directed a frowning stare at Jenna. 'But I insist. You have come all this way.'

Jenna gave a weak smile. 'Well, it wasn't all that far.'

Marina turned her whole body now, to face Jenna. 'The food will go to waste if you do not eat it. It is prepared.' Her words were stiff, as stiff as her expression.

'Right, I see.' Jenna meekly sat down again. Why, oh why, had she agreed to this? Marina clearly resented her being here.

Jenna sat alone, in the darkened room, smarting from the older woman's undisguised hostility. What a contrast to all the other Maltese people she'd met. They'd been welcoming, hospitable, going out of their way to make her feel at home — well, apart from Nicholas, that is. She grinned wryly to herself as she looked around the room, free to do so in greater detail now that she was alone. Mind you, she couldn't see very much, it was so gloomy.

She could see all the photos, however. Actually, she couldn't miss them. They occupied every possible surface, all framed, some ornately, some more plainly. Jenna couldn't resist, she stood up and walked over to one large grouping on a table. Each one, she saw, was of Marc. From the time he'd been a baby, right up to the present day. Nobody else featured. Just Marc. She picked up several, in order to study them more closely.

A trickle of unease crept through Jenna. Obsession? Or simply a mother's boundless love? It was obvious from these that, despite her show of disapproval, Marina adored her son.

Jenna wandered over to another cluster of frames. There was one here of Marina with Marc. Marc looked about two years old. He was dressed in a frilly cream shirt and short blue trousers, and he was sitting on his mother's knee. She picked this one up also, hoping she wasn't being too nosy.

The object of her interest wasn't Marc this time, but Marina. Just as she'd suspected, she'd been a beautiful woman, with long, rippling black hair and a warm smile. So the blonde was artificial. The years had been relatively kind to her, but, comparing the present day person to the one in this photo, it was clear that hardness had replaced warmth. Could that be due to the man she loved abandoning her? It seemed more than likely.

Her figure, Jenna noted, had also thickened over the years, turning from voluptuous to buxom. She found herself wondering about Marc's father. Was there anything of him in Marc?

He had his mother's dark hair, but that was all. His straight nose and chiselled jawline must have been inherited from his father. Marina's nose was tip-tilted, and her chin softer and rounder than Marc's.

As she stared at the photo of the two of them together, something fleetingly stirred, a recollection, a look, there was something familiar.

She shook her head. No. It was gone.

The door opened behind her. Swiftly, she returned to her chair. She didn't want them to catch her snooping. Marc and his mother came in. Marc was pushing a fully laden tea trolley, Marina was holding a large teapot.

'I know how you English like your tea,' she said, somehow managing to make it sound like a failing on Jenna's part. 'Your father was the same. It always had to be tea. That or vodka and tonic.' She sniffed again. She clearly hadn't approved of Vince's drinking habits.

'You knew my father well?'

Marina busied herself laying out plates and cups and saucers on a low table in the centre of the room.

'Not really, no. I made him tea when I worked for him. We weren't close, not like you and Marc.' She gave another sniff.

Jenna wondered what she was supposed to say to that? She also wondered exactly what Marc had been telling his mother? Jenna looked at him. He was starting to appear every bit as uncomfortable as Jenna was feeling.

The scarlet tinge was once more rising up his face as he spoke. 'Well, I wouldn't describe us as close,' Jenna haltingly began.

'Wouldn't you? That's not what I've been hearing.'

'Mama!' Marc faintly reproved her,

at the same time smiling apologetically at Jenna. He held out a plate of beautifully cut sandwiches. Each one was trimmed into a perfect triangle.

'Marc has taken you out.' Marina swung towards her son. 'Marc — you told me.'

'Well, just the once, when I first arrived. Marc was kind enough to . . . '

'Yes, well, Marc has always been a kind boy. That is the way I brought him up. People tend to sometimes — um, misinterpret his intentions.'

And she looked meaningfully at Jenna.

Jenna felt a surge of indignation. 'I don't believe I have misinterpreted anything.'

Marina's one eyebrow lifted. 'No?'

'No. Marc and I are just friends, no more.'

Again, she gave that annoying sniff. 'Yet, you are here today.' This time it was the raised eyebrow — again. 'To meet his mother.'

Really, what was the matter with this

woman? Was she this suspicious with everyone — or was it just her, Jenna? I mean, she'd heard of protective mothers, but this was ridiculous. 'Yes, because Marc said that you had known my father and wished to meet me, his daughter.'

'Really! Is that what Marc said?' Marina clearly didn't believe her. 'I noticed you looking at my photographs.'

So, she hadn't been quick enough returning to her seat. Still, she hadn't been doing anything wrong. 'Yes, they're all of Marc.'

'Marc is my life, Miss Saliba.'

'Oh, please, call me Jenna.' Now why had she said that? The very last person she wanted to become friends with was this — this critical woman.

'Miss Saliba.' It was said quite deliberately and with marked emphasis. She wanted it known that she had no intention of fostering any sort of closeness with her son's employer. 'I would do anything to protect him, to give him what he deserves.'

With that, she did what she had so far refused to and smiled, directly at Jenna. It was a slow, cat-like smile, her mouth a thin line, her eyes almost closed. There was not a shred of warmth in it.

Jenna shivered. Was that some sort of veiled threat; a warning, maybe? 'Marc says that you didn't really know your father. What do you remember of him?'

This direct question caught Jenna unawares. 'Oh well, now let me see. Not very much, really. I was very young when he left. I remember him as a kind man, a gentle man, a loving father.'

'And your mother? What kind of woman was she?'

Jenna wondered why she'd asked the question if she wasn't interested in the answer.

And she clearly wasn't, if the manner in which she'd cut Jenna off was anything to go by.

'Just a normal woman.' What could she say? That her mother had driven her father away because he was too old? She'd die first. 'A good mother, and wife.'

'Really?' The single word was a contemptuous one. 'Yet your father left her — and you. And had no further contact with you.'

So, Marc did tell her some things, Jenna thought, if she knew that.

'Or you with him. Not the actions of a loving man, surely? Did you never wonder why?'

'Yes, of course I did. But I'm sure Marc will have told you,' Jenna allowed a little sarcasm to lace her words and tone, 'I believed he was dead.'

'Yes, Marc did tell me.'

Oh, so Marc had told her that too? Not bad for a son who, according to Marina, didn't tell her anything.

'Why would your mother have told you such a thing? Deprived you of your father? Such a cruel thing to do to your child.'

'Mama,' Marc whispered, 'please . . .'

But Marina ignored him. Her gaze

246

was riveted upon Jenna.

'I — I don't know.' She did, of course, but she wasn't about to share that information with this coldly critical woman. And it was none of her business, in any case. So why all these questions? What was it to her? She'd admitted she barely knew Vince . . .

'Look, I'm sorry.' She replaced her plate on the table and stood up. She'd had more than enough — both of this woman and her food. Another mouthful would choke her, for sure. 'I have to go.'

Marc leapt to his feet too. 'Jenna, please. Mama is too nosy — she doesn't mean anything.'

'It's not that.'

'Then what is it, Miss Saliba? Have I made you nervous? I apologise.'

'Marc.' Jenna looked pleadingly at the young man. There was something about his mother, something deeply unsettling; disturbing, even. She was loath to describe it as threatening, but that's how it was beginning to feel. This woman disliked her for some reason.

Maybe even hated her?

'Please, would you call me a taxi?'

'Certainly not.' This was Marina speaking. 'Marc will . . . '

But before she could complete whatever it was she was about to say, there was a loud knock on the front door, and then it opened and a female voice called, 'Hello, Marc? Marina?'

A broad smile illuminated Marina's face, at the exact second that Marc's expression darkened and he demanded, 'Mama, what have you done?'

'Stay Away From Him'

Marina ignored her son's question and called, 'We're in the sitting room, Gabriella. Please come in.'

A girl walked into the room, well, skipped in, really. She looked about Marc's age, maybe a little younger. She was dark haired, and dark eyed, as so many Maltese people were, and very pretty. 'Hi, how nice to see you both. Oh, I am sorry.' She spoke directly to Marina, 'I thought when you asked me to come that it would be just you and Marc — I didn't realise you'd have company.'

The expression on her face, however, gave the lie to that. Jenna suspected that she'd known precisely who would be here. Her slanting glance at the older woman confirmed this impression. They were patently in cahoots.

'Oh, don't mind that,' Marina breezily assured her, looking, for the first time that afternoon, happy. 'Gabriella, this is Jenna Saliba. Marc works for her at the hotel.'

The girl swung to face Jenna then, her mouth widening into a smile. A smile that didn't reach her eyes. She held out a hand, a tiny, daintily manicured hand. Jenna took it. The girl herself was tiny, more like a child.

'Gabriella is Marc's girlfriend,' Marina smugly told her.

'Mama,' Marc burst out. 'You know that is not true.'

Marina turned stony eyes upon her son. 'Since when?'

'Well, um,' Marc couldn't seem to meet his mother's gaze.

'Since he met Miss Saliba,' Gabriella coolly interrupted him. 'Isn't that right, Marc?'

'Don't be silly, Gabriella,' Marina said, 'Miss Saliba and Marc are just good friends. Miss Saliba herself has said so.' Her subsequent stare challenged Jenna to contradict that statement.

It was as Jenna had suspected. Marina didn't want some older English woman waltzing in and stealing him away. She wanted Gabriella for him, a girl of his own age, a Maltese girl. That's what all the hostility had been about. It was nothing to do with Jenna herself.

Marina had plans for her only son. And she had invited Gabriella here to illustrate that. The trouble was it didn't look as if Marc agreed with those plans. Otherwise why end his relationship with Gabriella?

Determined to set the record straight, once and for all, Jenna said, 'Yes,' she smiled warmly, directly at the girl, 'we are just friends. Marc has been very kindly helping me to settle in here, haven't you, Marc?' She now smiled straight at Marc, hoping he would read her signal and agree with her.

'Yes,' he muttered, somewhat ungraciously.

'Well, that is good,' Gabriella smiled again, it still didn't reach her eyes, they

remained like pebbles; shiny, hard —
until she looked at Marc, that was.

It was quite clear to Jenna that she
was in love with Marc, or thought she
was. Her whole face lit up as she looked
at him, her eyes lost their unpleasant
hardness and shone. Jenna bit at her
bottom lip. They were very young to be
making up their minds about a lifetime
partner. Although, she doubted that
Marc had done that.

Gabriella glanced back at Jenna.
Uncertainty clouded her eyes. She
wasn't convinced that Jenna had no
interest in Marc. Jenna tried to reassure
her with another even warmer smile.

'Gabriella, please sit down and have
some tea with us. Marc, hand around
the sandwiches, please.' Marina began
to pour tea for Gabriella. 'Miss Saliba,
more tea?' she politely asked.

'No, really, I must go. There's no
need for Marc to take me. If he could
call a taxi for me . . . '

There was no argument this time.
Marina simply looked at her son and

said, 'Marc, please call a taxi for Miss Saliba.'

'But, Mama, I will take her . . . '

'No, Marc. You will stay and entertain Gabriella. She has come especially to see you.'

'Yes, Mama.'

Jenna couldn't help but see the glance that passed between the other two women; it was one of triumph. A swelling of pity for Marc engulfed her. What chance did he have? His mother would always dominate him, that was becoming clearer by the second. He'd end up with Gabriella, she was sure of that.

If only Marc's father had stayed. How different things might have been. For one thing, maybe Marc wouldn't be so firmly under his mother's thumb? A man, surely, would have intervened on his son's behalf, told his mother to leave him be — pointed out that she was smothering him beneath the shroud of maternal love?

Jenna gave a slight shiver. Marina was

a formidable woman. She wouldn't want to cross her. She dreaded to think what might happen if she was indeed romantically involved with Marc.

★　★　★

Nicholas was standing by the reception desk when Jenna arrived back. Good Lord, he hadn't been there all the time she'd been out, had he?

'Ah, Jenna.' His glance moved beyond her. 'No Marc then?'

'No, I took a taxi back. He'd got another visitor.'

'Oh?'

'Yes, a girl called Gabriella. She came to tea as well.'

'I see. His girlfriend?' His gaze glittered with speculation as it lingered upon her.

'She thinks so. I'm not sure whether Marc thinks that, though.'

'Hmmm. Bit tense, was it? That mother of his, well, let's just say she likes her own way.'

'Do you know her?'

'Not really. She's come here, demanding to speak to Marc once or twice. It's best to agree.' He shrugged. 'It might do Marc good to get out from under her influence. But,' he shrugged again, 'it's not really any of my business.'

'No.'

His face hardened. 'You might do well to keep your distance.'

'Yes, so you've said — more than once. And again, I say, we're just friends. Nothing more. He doesn't seem to have many of those.'

'Not surprisingly from what I've heard. His mother keeps them at bay, apparently. He should stand up to her, it's the only way.'

This was exactly what Jenna had been thinking. For once, their thoughts were perfectly attuned.

'Maybe,' he went on, 'if he'd had a father around — well, who knows. It might have been a whole different story.' His gaze darkened then, as he recalled that Jenna had been in just the same position. 'Sorry, that was a bit tactless.'

'Not at all. As opposed to Marc, I had a mother who let me have all the freedom I wanted.'

★ ★ ★

Jenna was still in her apartment the next morning when Bella phoned through on the house phone to say that there was someone here to see Jenna.

'Who is it, Bella?' she asked.

She heard the murmur of voices and then Bella said, 'Gabriella Bartello.'

'Take her into the small bar,' Jenna knew it would be empty at this time of the morning as it was only nine o'clock, 'I'll talk to her there.'

Jenna felt a small stab of apprehension. What on earth could Gabriella want to see her for? Had Marina sent her? To warn Jenna off Marc? Although, Marina had done that fairly successively herself.

Jenna, determined to hide her sense of misgiving, greeted Gabriella cheerfully. 'Good morning. This is a surprise. Can I offer you something? A cup of coffee? A cold drink?' She was babbling now, 'Some fruit juice?' Stop it, she firmly told herself. This was just a girl. She could handle her — whatever she'd come for.

'No, thank you. Nothing.'

'Then how can I help you? Marc's not in yet — at least not as far as I know.' She didn't want to give the impression that she and Marc were intimately acquainted with each other's movements.

'It is not Marc that I wish to see. I would have gone to his house if that were the case. I do know where he is.' And she smiled smugly. 'No, it is you I wish to speak to, Miss Saliba.'

'Oh, please, call me Jenna. Miss Saliba is so stuffy.'

The girl looked perplexed. 'Stuffy? What is that? I don't understand.'

'Sorry. I meant formal.'

The expression of confusion cleared. 'Ah, I see. Stuffy. Yes, I must remember that.'

Jenna was bemused. She really was like a child. She even dressed like a child. She was wearing a pair of dark blue denim bib and braces shorts and a T-shirt.

Her long hair was tied back with a matching blue ribbon. Her face was completely devoid of make up. Her skin looked scrubbed and shiny — just as a small girl's would have. 'So what is it you wish to see me about?' Jenna asked once more.

All of a sudden, the child-like innocence disappeared, to be replaced with an expression that could only be described as a mixture of cunning and hostility. It was a remarkable transformation. 'It's about Marc.'

'I told you, Marc and I are just friends.'

'That may be true for you. I don't think it is for Marc.'

Jenna shrugged. 'Well, I can't help

that. I have never encouraged him.'

'That isn't true, though, is it?' Gabriella spat. 'You have encouraged him all the time. Right from the first day you arrived. Did you know, that within a week of you being here, he had ended things with me? Told me to stay away from him. He wanted nothing to spoil what you two had.'

'What we had!' Jenna cried. 'We didn't have anything, and still don't.'

Gabriella inched closer, thrusting her face almost into Jenna's, close enough for Jenna to feel her breath.

'You have had your claws in him from day one. You are all he talks about. It is Jenna this and Jenna that.' Her mouth twisted into an ugly sneer.

'I didn't know that.' Which wasn't strictly true. She had feared that Marc was becoming too attached to her. Evidently, she'd been right to fear that. No wonder Marina had been so antagonistic. If he'd also talked like that to his mother?

'I want you to stay away from him.'

Jenna gave a little snort of laughter. 'A bit difficult to do as he works for me.'

It was the wrong thing to say. Gabriella's expression changed instantly, from hostility to downright dangerous. She moved yet closer. Their faces were almost touching. Jenna took a step back. It was silly, but she felt threatened. Yet, Gabriella was too small to do any real damage, wasn't she? It was then that she wondered whether this girl could have had in hand in her *accidents*? But how? How would she have known where she was? Would Marc have told her? Maybe she'd asked him?

'Dismiss him.'

'What?'

'Dismiss him. You can do that, can't you? You are the big boss, as you English say.'

'I can't just dismiss him without very good reason.'

'Why not? Tell him his services are no longer required. You have enough staff.'

'No. I would have to consult with Mr Portelli.'

'Oh, so you are not the big boss?'

'Mr Portelli and I are partners. We take decisions together, especially decisions about staff.'

'So tell him what you want to do. I'm sure he will agree. He doesn't like Marc — Marc has told me. He doesn't like Marc chasing around after you.'

How much had Marc told her? Jenna wondered. Quite a lot by the sound of it. Which meant they must still be fairly close, must see something of each other. Not quite the picture she'd painted just moments ago, the one in which Marc had told her to stay away from him.

'Marc thinks you and he will become romantically involved.'

Jenna gasped. 'I can assure you he's not had that from me. I have never led him to think . . . '

'No? You even went to meet his mother. Why would you do that? Unless you had some idea of a relationship?'

'No. It wasn't like that. Marc said his mother had asked to meet me. She had known my father. That's the only reason I went.'

'You are saying Marc lied to you?'

'Yes — no. Oh, I don't know. I don't know who to believe. But one thing I do know, I have no wish to start a relationship with Marc.'

'Have you told him that?'

'Well, not in so many words, but I haven't actually encouraged him.' But, of course, she had. Dancing with him in the way she had, flirting with him. Using him to disguise her distress — her jealousy, even — over the way Nicholas had behaved with Pauline. A deep sense of shame engulfed her.

'Well, please tell him, and then stay away from him. If you don't . . . '

'What?'

'Things could get a little unpleasant.' And with that, she whirled and almost ran from the bar.

Jenna stood quite still. What did that mean? Things could get a little unpleasant? Was she threatening Jenna? With what? Another accident? She'd have to speak to Marc, let him know, in no uncertain terms, that she was no interested in him.

But her nerve failed her. She couldn't tell him to stay away from her. She couldn't be that cruel. She would do as Gabriella had said. She'd keep her distance. Play it cool and hope he got the message.

*　　*　　*

After having to deal with Gabriella, she found she couldn't face Marc. She knew he was working today; he was due in at ten. She'd take the day off, go out somewhere. Take a walk, admire the countryside. Anything but stay here. It was the coward's way, she freely admitted, but she couldn't help that.

It was as she was leaving the hotel via the main entrance that she spotted Gabriella again. The girl was hanging around outside — waiting for Marc?

Jenna raised a hand in greeting but Gabriella ignored her.

She turned and began to walk in the opposite direction. It led to a pretty spectacular coastal path, according to Bella, and, as yet, she hadn't explored it. Now might be a good time to do just that.

Jenna walked briskly, taking care where she stepped, because the ground was pretty rough and quite stony. The last thing she wanted was to trip and fall. The views were glorious, just as Bella had said and the sky was that intense blue that you never see in England, the sort of blue that made it difficult to distinguish where the sky ended and the sea began.

A sound from behind made her turn. It had sounded like the scuffle of someone tripping over a stone. There was no-one there, however, so she carried on walking.

A second noise made her whirl once again, and this time she thought she saw something — something just beyond a large boulder to one side of the path.

She shivered with nervousness and waited for a moment or two. If someone had been there, they'd have to come out. When no-one reappeared, she decided she must have imagined it. She was getting paranoid and was it any wonder after the events of the past few hours?

The sun was getting hotter by the second. She pulled her sun hat from her bag and rammed it down on to her head. Out of the corner of her eye she saw something again, this time a mere blur of movement. Nothing definite, nothing she could possibly identify. It had been gone again as quickly as it had appeared.

A bird called then from nearby; she saw it fly away, its wings noisily beating the air. How pathetic was that? Allowing herself to be spooked by a bird. But maybe it was understandable. Birds were such a rare sight on Malta. She decided to cut short her walk and return to the hotel. She was too jumpy, too strung out to enjoy it. If she bumped into Marc, so be it. She'd have to cope.

It was as she was passing the boulder again that she saw something lying on the ground. She walked over to it and looked down. It was a woman's lace edged handkerchief. She picked it up and then glanced around. So, she was right. There had been someone here. But where had they gone? She saw then what she hadn't noticed before, another path — well, a track, really, one that led off at right angles to the path she was on. Whoever had dropped this must have gone that way.

Could it have been Gabriella? Following her to see where she was going? Or had her intention been more malevolent? The cliffs here were quite high. One push and she'd be over, straight down on to the rocks below. Memories of her other accidents returned, and a stab of fear made itself felt. She had to get back,

back to where she'd feel safe.

She started to run, her heartbeat accelerating wildly. It was a mistake. Her foot landed clumsily on a large stone. Her ankle twisted beneath her and she fell sideways, hitting the hard ground with an ominous thud as she did so.

A Terrifying Encounter

Jenna lay on the stony ground, gasping, terrified she'd hurt herself. She was far enough away from the hotel to make it difficult, if not impossible, to walk back unassisted if she really had injured her ankle.

Gingerly, she sat up and moved her foot. It hurt. Her elbow was stinging too. She lifted her arm, the better to see it. It was quite badly grazed, but not actually bleeding. It was her ankle that worried her. Cautiously, carefully, she got to her feet. It felt OK. She took a step. A pang of pain provoked a low groan, but it was nothing that would prevent her from walking.

She glanced around fearfully. Someone had been behind her. Stalking her? Trying to frighten her? Or more seriously, about to hurt her? Mercifully, whoever it had been seemed to have gone. She stood still and listened. All she could hear were the sounds she expected to hear, the synchronised buzzing of the cicadas, the distant call of a lone gull.

Slowly, watching where her feet landed to ensure she didn't tread on another stone and fall a second time, she made her way back to the hotel, all the time keeping a close watch out for anyone following behind.

It seemed hours to a frightened Jenna before the hotel loomed into view. There was no sign of Gabriella outside. That, at least, was something to be thankful for. She couldn't have stood to be harangued again. The sheer effort of getting back had exhausted her and her ankle was aching quite badly now.

Columbus greeted her in his usual exuberant manner with a piercing wolf whistle. Jenna breathed a sigh of relief; she was safe.

'Jenna.'

It was Marc. Jenna drew a deep breath. She must start as she meant to go on. She gave a quick wave and began to walk away in the direction of her and Nicholas's office, desperately trying to hide her limp from him.

But he wasn't about to be evaded that easily. 'Jenna,' he called again, more insistently this time.

Jenna couldn't do anything else but stop. 'Yes, Marc. What is it?' She kept her tone business-like and curt.

'Jenna, I'm really, really sorry about yesterday. I don't know what got into my mother.'

Jenna looked directly at him. 'Don't you, Marc?'

'No. She's not normally that — unfriendly.'

'She feels threatened.'

'What on earth do you mean?'

'You've obviously given her to understand that there is much more between you and I than there is.'

He did have the grace to blush slightly. 'Can I help it if she's misinterpreted what I said?'

'You should have put her straight,

Marc. And then there's Gabriella. She's been to see me this morning.'

'What!'

'To warn me away from you.'

'No!' he exclaimed. 'How dare she?'

'She's in love with you, Marc. That's why she dares. I think you and I should stay away from each other.'

'No. How can you say such a thing? I will not be dictated to by a couple of jealous women.' He began to stride back and forth, his hands thrust into his trouser pockets, his brow lowered as he gave her a black glare. 'And you — who do you think you are? Just deciding to brush me off! Don't I mean anything to you?'

'Jenna, is everything OK?'

It was Nicholas. Jenna turned to him in relief.

'Farruq, shouldn't you be laying the tables for lunch?' It was unmistakable dismissal.

Marc didn't respond for a moment, but then he muttered, 'Yes,' before hunching his shoulders and stomping

away, still muttering darkly, thus con-
forming Jenna's view that he was still
little more than a teenage boy. Jenna
watched him go, her expression a
deeply troubled one.

Nicholas asked, 'What the devil was
going on then?'

'It was just Marc venting his rage
about the women in his life. It was
nothing I can't deal with.'

But, despite her words, Jenna wasn't
sure about that. There had been
something almost unbalanced about
Marc in those few seconds. Something
she hadn't seen before. She'd stay out
of his way for a while, give him time to
calm down.

'Well, if he gives you any more
trouble, you let me know. He'll get his
marching orders.'

* * *

Over the next day or two, Jenna's
twisted ankle mended, even if her fear
that it could have been Gabriella

following her refused to go away. However, as she saw nothing further of the girl, she did eventually manage to forget about her. Especially when it became evident that Nicholas was mellowing towards her. Mainly, she suspected, because she was rigorous about maintaining a respectable distance from Marc.

Gradually, very gradually, Nicholas's manner grew more as it had been when she first arrived. There was still a slight reserve about him, but this thawing of his frosty demeanour eventually inspired her to say, 'Nicholas, I really would like to explain what you saw with Rick.'

That incident had replayed itself in her head repeatedly, as had the look that had wreathed Nicholas's face as he'd stared down at her. It needed to be cleared up, and then put behind them. Until that happened, there was no chance of any sort of relationship developing between them. Personal or professional.

'You don't owe me an explanation,' he coolly said. 'Anyway, it's long over and done with. And as you said once before, what you do in your own time is your business.'

'I really would like to explain,' she insisted. 'Please.'

He shrugged, his broad shoulders moving beneath the fine texture of his shirt, the sheer masculinity of him only too apparent. Jenna suppressed a small shiver of longing. Pauline had been right, of course. She was attracted to him, powerfully attracted.

'OK,' he agreed. 'Let's have dinner tonight. Somewhere away from this place.' He glanced around, almost contemptuously. 'Too many cocked ears here.'

He was referring to Marc, she suspected. Despite his flare of temper and rudeness the other day, he'd begun to hang around her once more. He seemed to be everywhere she looked, his smile ingratiating, his eyes warmly admiring.

She'd tried to be as off-putting as she could, but it didn't seem to be working. If Gabriella should get wind of it? Well, who was to say what would ensue.

Sooner or later Jenna would again have to say something to him about it. And she wasn't looking forward to it. Because whenever she looked at Marc, she also saw his mother. And, for whatever reason, she'd definitely felt uneasy in her company.

In fact, she was beginning to feel positively besieged and intimidated. It wasn't a feeling she cared for, so she welcomed Nicholas's suggestion that they go somewhere other than the hotel's dining room.

'I know a very good restaurant, The Trocadero. It has a balcony overlooking the sea. We could sit at one of the tables out there. It's set quite high up so it should feel cooler.'

As the last few days had been exceptionally hot, the sun relentlessly beating down without even the smallest breeze, Jenna knew a sense of relief.

Oh, what heaven it would be to feel cool again.

'You don't suffer from vertigo, do you?' Nicholas enquired, clearly as an afterthought.

'No.'

'Good. I'll see you later then.'

As he walked away with that easy stride that she was so familiar with by this time, the stride that invariably set her pulses racing, Jenna's spirit soared. Things were going to be all right, she was sure.

★ ★ ★

However, what she hadn't expected was that Marc would also ask her out that evening. This was her chance to say something, to make it clear that his pursuit of her had to stop.

'I can't, Marc, I'm sorry. Nicholas and I are going to The Trocadero. Business to discuss. And maybe it would be better for everyone if you stopped following me around. You have a lovely girl who wants you, a girl your own age,' she lamely said. 'I'm sorry to have to say it, but this pursuit of me, well, it isn't appropriate and,' she braced herself for his anger, 'it isn't what I want.'

His features darkened, his eyes narrowed. She knew what was coming. She should do, she'd been on the receiving end of his venom a few times now.

'Well,' he spat, 'I hope you know what you're doing as far as Nicholas Portelli is concerned. Heaven knows, I've tried to warn you often enough.' But then, almost at once, he plastered a broad smile upon his face and it was as if the black mood and vicious words had never been. 'We'll have to go out another night,' and he coolly walked away.

Jenna stared at him. That was a first. His moods were changeable, but she'd never seen it happen that fast. His black mood usually lasted a good day or so. Not for the first time, she wondered if there was something wrong with him?

Bella had been standing nearby and had raised her eyebrows at Jenna after Marc went. She said, 'His mother's obsessed with him, spoils him, treats him like a little boy. Always has done. This is the result of doing all his thinking for him. He can't take rejection.'

As Jenna couldn't and didn't want to say she wholeheartedly agreed with Bella, having witnessed Marina's behaviour with her son at first hand, she said, 'Maybe she's simply tried to make up for him not knowing his father? With no other male presence in their lives, she's tried to be both mother and father to him.'

'Hmm, maybe. But he really shouldn't speak to you like that. Good job Nicholas wasn't around to hear him. He'd have been sacked on the spot.'

The same thought had already occurred to Jenna. In fact, the thought that she herself should have taken the opportunity to sack him had also occurred to her.

★　★　★

That evening, Jenna dressed with care. She had to make things right with Nicholas but the prospect of trying to do that worried her. Maybe she was wasting her time? Maybe he didn't care about the truth of what had happened between her and Rick?

Although, Pauline had seemed sure that he was attracted to her. Jenna, on the other hand, wasn't at all confident. And yet, he'd kissed her that night at the barbecue and had clearly disliked her seeing Marc and Rick. She sighed. He was a complete enigma. All she did know was that it would be well-nigh impossible for them to go on working together if they didn't get things resolved between them.

This constant acrimony was beginning to wear her down. And the plain fact was, and there was no point in continuing to deny it, she was falling in love with him, more deeply with every day that passed. For a brief while, she'd believed he felt the same. She sighed again, now she didn't know what to believe.

After much chopping and changing of one outfit for another, she finally settled upon a plain cream dress with shoestring straps. She brushed her hair until it shone with burnished highlights and applied the minimum of make up. She glowed. And Nicholas's eyes, as she walked towards him, told her that she'd achieved what she'd set out to do.

'Ready?' he asked.

Jenna nodded. Her heart was beating so fast now, her breath had caught in her throat, making it impossible to speak.

'You look lovely.'

'Thank you.'

The sun was sinking, turning the horizon to a deep apricot and magenta, as they walked to his car, an expensive-looking silver Mercedes, parked in front of the hotel, and within minutes it seemed to Jenna they were pulling up outside The Trocadero. Bit different to riding on Marc's bike, she couldn't help but reflect; a darned sight quicker too, and definitely more comfortable.

A black suited waiter, obviously the maitre d', greeted Nicholas by name, and led them outside on to a broad balcony and a secluded, candlelit table for two. The air was perfumed and, as always, vibrating with the song of the cicadas. Thick vines intertwined overhead, broken only by dozens of minute lights threaded through the leaves. Just as Nicholas had promised they were high enough to look out over miles and miles of sea, and the breeze was gloriously cooling after the heat of the day.

Jenna, unable to resist it, walked to the edge of the balcony and leaned over the iron balustrade. The sea gently lapped rocks many, many feet below.

'Careful,' it was Nicholas speaking from right behind her, 'one slip and you could be over.'

Jenna shuddered, her fears resurrected in a single instant. There hadn't been any more *accidents* if you excluded her fall on the cliff top walk the day she thought she was being followed. And that couldn't possibly have been Nicholas. Or could it?

She'd assumed it was Gabriella because of the woman's handkerchief that she'd found. But that could have been dropped at some other time by someone else. What if it had been Nicholas who'd followed her from the hotel?

Was that why he'd brought her here? Not to listen to her explanation of what had truly happened between her and Rick, but to murder her? Had she heedlessly walked into his trap? She took a step backwards, right into his arms, they wrapped themselves around her, his hands clasping at the front of her waist.

Jenna gasped. Was this it? She glanced backwards. They were the only people here. He could so easily lift her, tip her over the balustrade.

She stiffened and Nicholas instantly

released her. His glance at her was a strange one. Jenna felt her heart race, her breathing quicken. Had he realised she was on to him? If it was him? No, she couldn't believe it; wouldn't believe it.

'Come on. I've ordered some wine,' and he led her back to the table. Those few words banished her fear, making everything seem ordinary and commonplace. She was being ridiculous. He'd hardly have brought her to a restaurant to kill her. There were other much more appropriate places. Places where no-one could possibly witness what he was doing.

She tried to calm herself. Just breathe. In, out, in out, she instructed herself, and gradually her heartbeat slowed, as did her breathing. She regarded him across the table. He met her gaze easily, confident and relaxed. Not the demeanour of someone planning murder. Yet — someone had heaved a brick at her on those cliff steps. Someone had toppled the pot from the balcony in the hotel, and someone had stalked her in the darkness of its gardens. And if not Nicholas, then who? Gabriella?

No, it wasn't possible. She wouldn't have had access to the hotel grounds. The cliff steps — yes. But would she have known about Jenna then? She'd only been in the hotel for a matter of hours. She'd barely even met Marc. He certainly wouldn't have had time to tell Gabriella about her. No, that first incident couldn't have been her. Stop it, she told herself for the umpteenth time. There was no proof that anyone had done anything. She was overreacting — again.

They sat down and the waiter poured their wine for them. Jenna watched Nicholas over the rim of her glass as she took a large gulp in an effort to slow the once more rapid beating of her heart. He stared back at her for a long, long moment before raising his glass to her, 'Here's to a long and happy partnership. To us,' he said in a low, throaty voice.

What did that mean? To us? Jenna felt her breath catching in her throat again, with the consequence that when she also said, 'To us,' it erupted as a high pitched squeak. She saw the twitch of Nicholas's lips as he struggled to suppress a grin.

'Sorry,' she gasped, 'I'll try again. Some wine must have gone the wrong way. To us.' Thankfully, this time, it sounded perfectly normal.

The evening progressed easily and so amicably that Jenna almost forgot the reason she wanted to talk to him. Nicholas skilfully drew her out and she found herself talking about her life in England, about the letters she'd found and subsequently read in her apartment, the photograph album.

'They looked so happy to start with,' she told him, 'but then you could see that everything went wrong. My mother . . . ' nervously she cleared her throat. Was it right to reveal the reasons for her parents' break up? Would she be betraying a confidence? ' ... had affairs. In his letter my father said he knew that and and he couldn't stand it. He was a lot older than her, as you probably realised.' Nicholas understood what had happened, she could tell.

He stretched out a hand across the table to her. Jenna gladly took it. Tears stung her eyes, just as they had when she'd read the despairing letters.

'I'm sorry, Jenna. It must have been very distressing for you to read about that.'

'Yes, it was.' She cleared her throat again. She'd tell him the truth about Rick, right now. While he was looking at her in that tender, understanding way. 'Um, about Rick ... '

'You don't have to say anything. It's nothing to do ... '

'Yes, yes, I do,' she cut in, 'and it is to do with you — if that's what you were going to say.' Nicholas nodded, confirming her belief. 'I want everything straight between us.'

Nicholas's one eyebrow lifted. Jenna

felt her heart miss a beat. It was a gesture she'd grown to love. Just as she loved him. Maybe he'd never feel the same way, but she could at least admit the truth to herself.

'Rick tried to force himself on me.'

Nicholas's fingers tightened painfully about hers. She winced. 'He what?' His expression darkened, his jaw hardening into steel, his eyes turning treacly. 'Why, in the Lord's name, didn't you say something that night? I'm so sorry for what I said. I should have known.'

'It's OK. Nothing actually happened between us. You turned up, fortunately, and saved me.' She gave a wry smile. 'Although it didn't seem that way at the time.'

'My Lord! I'm glad he's not around now because he and I would have a few things to sort out.' His glance sharpened. 'You're not going to see him again, are you? Either here or in England?'

She shook her head. 'No, it's unlikely I'll ever see him again. He knows now it's over for good. And I doubt I'll be returning to England any time in the near future. My life is here now.'

Nicholas didn't respond to that; he simply tilted his head to one side and watched her.

'Um . . . ' there was something she needed to know but was nervous about asking him, 'and you. Is there someone special in your life?' How would she feel if he said yes? Maybe it would be better not to know? However, she'd asked now so she'd have to take the consequences. Whatever they were.

'Oh yes,' he gave a slow smile, a sensual smile, 'someone very, very special.'

Jenna felt her heart turn right over. Well, she'd asked and now she knew. A feeling of unutterable misery engulfed her. There was no chance for her. A weird sense of almost detachment suffused her then. Her natural defences protecting her, shielding her from an excess of pain? Who was the lucky woman?

The maitre d' came to the table. 'I'm sorry to interrupt,' he spoke to Nicholas in English, out of courtesy to her, Jenna presumed, although everyone on this island spoke perfect English; along with Maltese it was their national language, 'but a gentleman is asking to see you outside, Mr Portelli.'

'Really? How strange. Did he give his name?'

'I'm sorry, no. The waitress who spoke to him foolishly didn't ask.' He shrugged his shoulders. 'Do you want me to find out?'

'No, no. That's all right. I'll come and see, although I can't imagine who would come here to see me rather than the hotel. And who would know I was here, come to that.' He turned to Jenna with an apologetic smile.

She didn't respond; she couldn't. After that fleeting sense of detachment, she felt too heartsick to do anything, other than think — maybe she should simply throw in the towel and return to England after all? Give Nicholas her shares. Leave him to his romance? It's what he wanted, after all.

He glanced back at the maitre d'. 'Right, I'll go out then. Jenna,' he turned to her again, 'I'll only be a moment.' He frowned. 'I can't imagine who it can be, but whoever it is can come and see me at the hotel tomorrow.'

As she watched him walk away from her, she wondered how she could have been so foolish? Of course a man like Nicholas Portelli would have a woman in his life. He'd probably had dozens over the course of the past few years. He had everything going for him, after all. Good looks, wealth and charm when he could be bothered to turn it on. Why on earth had she thought he'd be free for her?

She stood up and with tears stinging her eyes walked to the edge of the balcony, there were two other couples sitting at tables now, albeit a good distance from Jenna. However, as she didn't want to be seen weeping for what might have been, she concealed herself to one side of a particularly dense hibiscus bush. That and the deepening darkness provided the perfect screen. No-one would be able to see her or hear her.

Once there, she surrendered totally to her unhappiness and silently wept. Finally, finally, she'd met the one man she could love and he was involved with another woman. In love with her, obviously — if that smile was any indication.

Something rustled behind her, the branches of the bush shook, one struck her across the cheek, another caught in her hair. 'Hey, watch it,' she said.

'Jenna?' The word was softly spoken, so softly it was little more than a hiss.

Jenna peered into the bush. 'Nicholas? Is that you?'

The fact that he had come looking for her in this hidden place was something of a comfort. Maybe all wasn't lost, after all? But how had he known she was here? She half turned, pushing the branches to one side. 'How did you . . . ?'

Before she could get a look at him, however, or say anything more, his hands shot out and encircled her throat, his fingers gently squeezing, forcing her to turn so that she was looking out to sea once more and not towards him.

'Wh-what are you doing? Don't . . . ' she gasped. She thought she heard a low laugh. 'Nicholas, this isn't funny.' She was indignant now. 'I know it's you.'

'I saw you try to hide yourself. Impossible. There's no hiding place for you. Not from me.'

'Nicholas, please.'

'Don't talk.' His voice was harsh; unrecognisable. His breath was hot on the back of her neck. It made a rasping sound. A terrifying sound. The first clammy finger of terror clutched at her then. Had her earlier alarm been some sort of premonition?

His next words told her they had

been. 'And don't call out. I can snap your neck with just one movement of my hands. It's so . . . ' he began to stroke it, even dropped a kiss on it, '. . . delicate. So,' the rasping was directly in her ear now; the strands of her hair moved as he breathed, 'if you don't want to suffer as you die, stay still. Just leave everything to me. It won't hurt. It will be over swiftly, I promise you that, but you have to die, it's the only way.'

Two Hearts Are Healed

Jenna's eyes widened as her heart raced in terror. She did as he said, too terrified to do anything else.

'Nicholas,' she gasped. Had he lost his mind? People would see, surely? Even hidden as they were by the bushes? 'Please don't do this. You don't need to . . . '

His hands tightened on her throat, severely constricting her breathing.

'This-this isn't funny.' She'd just had the crazy notion that he wasn't mad, he was just teasing her. She struggled to turn her head, wanting nothing more than to see him in that second. If he was serious and he was going to kill her, then she wanted to look into his eyes — see his expression as he did it.

'I'm sorry, Jenna, but I have to do this. I can't have you ruining things for me. It will be quick, I promise . . . '

'Aah, stop — please!' His fingers tightened again. Jenna felt the blood thickening behind her eyes. She was going to black out; he was going to kill her. The man she'd grown to love was actually going to kill her. Well, he was going to have to do it with her looking at him.

With one final, mighty effort, she succeeded in turning her head; her breath stilled in he throat at what she saw.

It wasn't Nicholas, it was Marc.

'Marc!' she croaked.

'That's right. It's me. This time you won't escape and Nicholas will be blamed for your death. Several of the staff saw you leave the hotel together. The maitre d' saw you here together. When your body is found, they'll all remember Vanessa. They'll say he murdered her because he needed her money, and now he's done the same to you because he wants your share of the hotel. He will go to prison.'

She was struggling to breathe, to

remain conscious, even though her thoughts were a maelstrom. 'B-but why? Why are you doing this? What have we ever done to you?' If she had to die, she, at least, wanted to know the reason why.

'Your father was also my father,' he hissed. 'He had a fling with my mother and left her pregnant with me. Left her . . . ' he shook her ' . . . alone.'

It explained everything: the way his child's face in the photograph had seemed familiar — it would, it had had the look of her father; the resentful hostility of his mother towards her, Vince's legitimate daughter; Marc's relentless pursuit of her; his close observation. He'd always known where she was and what she was doing. It would be so easy to follow her, get rid of her. Jenna could feel her life seeping from her. Her eyes began to close. His voice whispered in her ear, his voice low and full of evil intent.

'I was planning to tell everyone and claim half of the hotel when you turned up. No-one knew he had a daughter; no-one.'

'Ni-Nicholas knew,' she managed to say.

'Yes, Nicholas knew and he said nothing. You have taken what should have been mine.'

'I'll share my half with you.' She managed to gasp.

'No. A quarter is not enough, not when I can have it all.' He gave a low laugh. 'With you out of the way, and Nicholas,' he spat the name out, 'locked up, it can all be mine. It is my right as my father's only surviving heir.' His grip convulsed, shutting off the air almost completely.

But then, his grip loosened again and Jenna's eyes snapped open. She fought desperately to drag much needed air into her lungs. 'Bu-but why poison my mind against Nicholas?' she croaked. 'He'd done nothing.'

'I needed you to trust me and after the first failed attempt I didn't want you to suspect me. I reasoned that if I made you afraid of him, you'd turn to me. We'd become close, I'd know your every move. It would give me another opportunity of getting rid of you. I tried three times and each time I failed.'

'So, it was you,' she gasped. 'The steps, the pot in the garden.'

'Yes. And nothing worked,' he snarled, 'despite all my efforts. And then, then you told me I had to stay away from you. How would I have known what you were doing, where you were? I decided I had to act.' He tightened his grip on her throat. Jenna choked as she struggled desperately to breathe. 'And this time, I'm going to succeed. I'll be rid of both you and Nicholas once and for all.'

'Th-the maitre d' knows Nicholas is outside, that he couldn't possibly have done this.'

'The maitre d' is busy inside. He won't know whether Nicholas came back or not. No, he will get the blame.'

He was right, of course. And she was going to die. There was one last thing that Jenna needed to know, however.

'Did my father know about you? Th-that he had a son?'

'No, my mother kept it a secret — even from me. She only told me after he'd died.'

But Jenna didn't hear any more. She'd relinquished the fight for life and lapsed into unconsciousness, completely oblivious to Marc trying to heave her up and over the balustrade, his intention to fling her to the rocks below and certain death.

* * *

'Jenna, Jenna, please, please open your eyes! Stay with me. Look at me. Jenna. Jenna!' It was Nicholas, frantically trying to bring her back to consciousness, holding her close, his breath catching in his throat as he pleaded with her to look at him.

Jenna heard him through a dark mist. Her throat was aching so badly she could barely breathe, let alone speak. Eventually, though, she managed to open her eyes and croak, 'Nicholas — Marc, he tried to — he tried . . . '

'Oh, thank goodness, you're back with me. It's all right, don't try to speak. It's all taken care of, he's in safe keeping. He can't hurt you.'

Another man's voice spoke then. 'It's OK. The police and the ambulance are on their way.' It was the maitre d'. He looked as anxious as Nicholas was. Well, maybe not quite as much. Nicholas's face was the colour of parchment, his eyes as dark as the night.

'He-he tried to strangle me. Marc . . . '

'Sssh, I know, darling. Don't try to talk. The police will be here in a matter of moments. When I came back and looked for you, and found Marc trying to heave you over the balcony. Why did you hide yourself away? If you hadn't done that, he couldn't have tried to heave you over.' He bent his head to hers, burying his face in her tangled hair, his breathing fast and anguished. 'He must have deliberately lured me outside, to get me out of the way. I walked around for several minutes. He must have somehow managed to sneak in and he must have seen where you went.' He pulled Jenna even closer, holding her as if she were the most precious thing on the planet.

But all Jenna could think was that he'd called her *darling*, Nicholas had called her *darling*. It was worth everything simply to hear him say that. 'But what about someone special,' she whispered. 'Who's the someone special you spoke about?'

He smiled down at her, those intriguing gold flecks making their appearance. 'You, my love. Only you.' And very, very gently he kissed her.

'Oh, Nicholas.' She smiled up at him dreamily. Had Marc succeeded in his plan? Had she indeed died and gone to heaven? Or was this really happening? He kissed her again, she kissed him back. But there was something she had to tell him. 'Marc's my half brother.'

'Yes, he told me. He was ranting about the hotel being rightfully his, not yours or mine. Your father never knew about him.'

'I know. Nicholas, the other things, the plant pot, someone in the garden — they were him. And he kept trying to make me think it was you. He wanted to kill me and get you blamed and get rid of both of us so that the hotel would be his.'

'Ssh, ssh,' he gently said, 'you can tell me all of this later. Don't worry. Marc will be going to prison for a very long time, I suspect. He won't be able to hurt you ever again.'

Jenna was transported to hospital, where she was given every possible care. In fact, she was treated as if she were royalty. Nicholas's doing, she was sure. Her throat continued to ache but she was so happy that even that didn't bother her. When Nicholas turned up with his arms full of roses, her happiness was complete.

'How are you this morning, my love?' he tenderly asked her, as he took his time in kissing her.

'Happy. Totally, completely, rapturously happy.'

'Hmmm.' Those flecks appeared. She knew now what they signified; an emotion equal to hers. He kissed her again. 'I love you, Jenna.'

'I love you too, but . . . ' There was something she had to ask him. Someone she needed to know.

He lifted an eyebrow at her. Her heart melted with love for him. 'But what?'

'Your wife, Vanessa. Did-did you . . . '

A frown instantly lowered his brow. 'I know what you're going to ask me.'

'Do you?'

'Yes. Did I push her off the cliff steps?'

Jenna nodded. His expression was a grim one. Had she just ruined her chances of spending the rest of her life with him? Her heart thudded at the prospect of losing him now. Nothing else mattered but that they were together. Not his wife or what had happened. 'It doesn't matter, Nicholas.

I love you, that's all that matters.'

'No, you need to know, otherwise you'll always have doubts. I had no part in Vanessa's death. It's true, the police were suspicious about it at first and they did question me, but the evidence soon showed that it had been an accident; a tragic accident. There were clear marks that proved beyond any shadow of doubt that Vanessa had slipped, that she hadn't been pushed.' His frown deepened. 'Did Marc tell you about it?'

'Yes, after I'd fallen down the same set of steps.'

'What! When was this?'

So she told him what had happened. 'It was Marc, he admitted it, it was the start of it all.'

'My Lord!' Nicholas wrapped her in his arms.

'He said Vanessa's accident happened just in time for you to inherit her wealth and buy into my father's hotel. He said a man had been seen at the top of the steps just before she fell.'

'Hang on. What wealth?'

'Marc said she'd inherited half a million from her parents.'

'She didn't inherit anything like that. And what she did inherit, she quickly spent. And just for the record there was no man involved in her accident either. There was never any suggestion of that.' He paused, regarding her thoughtfully. 'The truth is, and I haven't told anyone else this, but we were on the point of separating when she died.'

'Oh.' Jenna was shocked in silence.

'We hadn't been getting on for some time. We'd married far too young. Vanessa wanted her freedom.'

'Nicholas, I'm sorry.'

'Don't be. We both felt the same way. Jenna, I also want you to know that I didn't need anyone else's money to buy a share in the hotel. I had more than enough money of my own. You can check that if you like. I'll get you all the documents relating to . . . '

'No, no,' she hastened to say, 'I believe you. And clearly Marc was lying. He needed to make me suspicious, as well as afraid of you. He wanted me to turn to him. That way, he'd always know where I was and could — could — ' She couldn't go on. Nicholas squeezed her hand. 'I'm sorry for asking you.'

'Don't be. It had to be cleared up. He could have killed you, he very nearly did kill you. If I hadn't come back and found you . . . ' The blood drained from Nicholas's face. 'Jenna, all that he's done is explained by the fact that Marc has some sort of personality disorder and has had it for quite some time it appears. His mother should have got treatment for him years ago. She must have know there was something wrong — even as a child, apparently, he was unstable. The police want to talk to you, obviously, but it sounds as if they'll be charging him with attempted murder.'

His gaze softened then. 'I think maybe his mother didn't want to share him with your father. She's always been very possessive of him, apparently. Obsessively so.'

Jenna nodded. She'd had the same thought during that uncomfortable meeting.

'Anyway, enough about him for now. I want to talk about us.' He slipped his arms around her and pulled her close. 'I want to ask you something, Jenna.'

'Yes?' She gazed up at him, wide-eyed.

He gazed at her, dropping a lingering kiss upon her lips. 'Will you marry me? Clearly, someone has to look after you.'

She sighed rapturously. 'Oh, Nicholas, of course I will.' Every doubt she'd ever had had gone. Nicholas's love was genuine. One look into his eyes told her that. He would never want to hurt her, never had — if only she'd known it.

THE END

We do hope that you have enjoyed reading this large print book.

Did you know that all of our titles are available for purchase?

We publish a wide range of high quality large print books including:
Romances, Mysteries, Classics
General Fiction
Non Fiction and Westerns

Special interest titles available in large print are:
The Little Oxford Dictionary
Music Book, Song Book
Hymn Book, Service Book

Also available from us courtesy of Oxford University Press:
Young Readers' Dictionary
(large print edition)
Young Readers' Thesaurus
(large print edition)

For further information or a free brochure, please contact us at:
Ulverscroft Large Print Books Ltd.,
The Green, Bradgate Road, Anstey,
Leicester, LE7 7FU, England.
Tel: (00 44) **0116 236 4325**
Fax: (00 44) **0116 234 0205**

THE TURNING POINT

Phyllis Mallett

Barbara Taylor is on holiday, incognito, at the hotel her company has recently failed to take over. There she meets Jim Farrell, the harassed owner, and his young daughter Leanne. Then, fate intervenes in their lives and undercurrents threaten them. Barbara becomes so involved with the family that telling the truth about herself could shatter her new-found happiness — but eventually, when all is revealed, she can only hope that love will be kind to her.

MISS PETERSON & THE COLONEL

Fenella Miller

Lydia Peterson is content to run her stud farm and remain single — she doesn't want the autocratic Colonel Simon Wescott interfering with her life. However, thrown together by a series of dramatic events, their lives become endangered, forcing them to reconsider their first impressions. Will Simon be able to compromise his duty to put King and country first, in order to save Lydia's life? Can she give up her independence and become a soldier's wife?

AN ARRANGED MARRIAGE

Beth James

It's 1820 in South Yorkshire, and Patricia Pickering is wealthy, but lonely. A young widow and inheritor of the Pickering Mill, she is also joint owner of the Flint mill with her cousin, Robert. Meanwhile, Lord Percy Alexander of Wakefield Hall, is responsible for its debts and the welfare of his two younger siblings. Though Robert has proposed marriage to Patricia, to benefit the running of both the mills, she finds that it's Lord Percy who's on her mind — after he'd nearly knocked her over!

WHERE THE HEART IS

Sue Moorcroft

Malta 1968: Sylvana Bonnici's parents are dubious about her dream of being a globetrotting wife to British army staff sergeant Rob Denton. Sure enough, when Rob is posted to Singapore, the army dictates that he must leave her behind. When Rob is finally offered the posting Sylvana has yearned for, he's no longer sure that it's what he wants. Sylvana's reaction shocks him, but it's a horrifying accident that proves home is where the heart is . . .

THE FAMILY AT FARRSHORE

Kate Blackadder

After breaking up with Daniel, archaeologist Cathryn Fenton quite happily travels to Farrshore in Scotland to work on a major dig. In the driving rain, she gives a lift to Canadian Magnus Macaskill, then finds that they both lodge at the same place. The dig goes well, with Magnus filming the proceedings for a Viking series. But trouble looms in Farrshore — starting when Magnus learns that his son Tyler is coming over from Canada to be with his dad . . .